Also by Charlotte Carter

Jackson Park

TRIP WIRE

ONE WORLD
BALLANTINE BOOKS
NEW YORK

TRIP WIRE

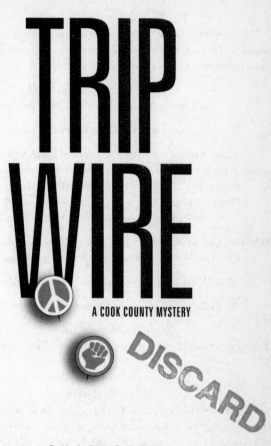

A COOK COUNTY MYSTERY

CHARLOTTE CARTER

A Strivers Row/One World Book
Published by The Random House Publishing Group

Copyright © 2005 by Charlotte Carter

One World Books website address: www.oneworldbooks.net

Library of Congress Cataloging-in-Publication Data

Carter, Charlotte (Charlotte C.)
Trip wire : a Cook County mystery / by Charlotte Carter.—1st trade pbk. ed.
p. cm.
Sequel to: Jackson Park.
ISBN 0-345-44769-7
1. Lincoln Park (Chicago, Ill.)—Fiction. 2. African American men—Crimes against—Fiction. 3. Interracial dating—Fiction. 4. Women detectives—Fiction. 5. Communal living—Fiction. 6. Chicago (Ill.)—Fiction. I. Title.

PS3553.A7736L56 2005
813'.54—dc22   2004052092

Manufactured in the United States of America

1 3 5 7 9 8 6 4 2

Text design by Susan Turner

First Edition: April 2005

TRIP WIRE

CHICAGO, 1968

THEY SAY HELL IS OTHER PEOPLE.

But what do they know?

Call me a reformed loner. After a lifetime of singleness, I am now living with a group of people almost any one of whom I would cut off an arm for.

We live in a tumbledown apartment that vibrates with the comings and goings of eight reasonably healthy young people living in their time. We study for exams, work shitty-paying gigs selling blue jeans or repairing bicycles, we talk about movies, bake bread, listen to records, and throw our hearts and bodies into the antiwar effort.

The demonstration at the Van Buren Street draft office today turned ugly, and thanks to the shiny billy clubs of Chicago's finest, one of the sweeter residents in our urban commune, Cliff

Tobin, has a fat lip. The rest of us proudly wear our assorted bruises. But we are all okay. We have made it back home.

Music is playing now, loud and defiant. One of our number is rolling enough good dope to cool out the state of Oklahoma. At the secondhand kitchen table, we will have a magnificent soup with root vegetables newly out of the earth, bum cigarettes, drink from one another's cups. Later in the night each of us will be somewhere in the city lying with a lover. Even me.

Even me, freckle-faced not-so-good-looking little black girl from the South Side, a happy recruit in the rock 'n' roll army of my generation, acid-dropping, yes to love, no to authority, eating life with a spoon, and whatever I was like last year, it's all different now.

Yes, I know: The world has been around a long time, doing just fine without us. We probably think way too much of ourselves. I don't care.

And anyway, it's almost Christmas.

CHAPTER ONE
MONDAY

"HEY, CASSANDRA," WILTON SAID IN THAT SLEEPY VOICE OF his.

"Huh?" I said.

"How much you bet me?"

"About what?"

"I bet you and me are the onliest niggers in Chicago know every song on the Creedence Clearwater album."

"No bet. I know we are."

We fell out laughing.

Truth to tell, I had nothing against Creedence and neither did Wilton. But our friend and roommate Dan Zuni, a beautiful Pueblo Indian kid with a mane of coal-black hair and the slim-hipped build of a female fashion model, had a psychotic thing for them. Night and day he had Creedence on the record player in his bedroom. Once in a while I had to beg for mercy. He was always nice enough to give it a rest when I complained, but a couple of hours later "Suzie Q" would be blasting again.

Wilton had me laughing so hard my ribs ached. But that wasn't such a tough assignment. I was stoned—we both were—and just about everything was funny.

We lay side by side on the floor of my room, only a couple of feet away from the new space heater my uncle Woody had paid for. Winter in Chicago is nothing to trifle with. You might think you know about our winters because of that record Lou Rawls had where he referred to the wind whipping off Lake Michigan as the Hawk. Don't kid yourself. You don't know. At night my room was like the north face of Everest. But I was low on cash, so Woody sprang for the heater, despite his being none too pleased with me these days.

Uncle Woody loved me, no question. But I had recently left home, moved out of the spacious high-rise apartment in Hyde Park where I had lived with him and my aunt Ivy since I was eleven years old. They were pretty pissed about it.

Maybe it wouldn't have been such an affront if I'd taken a nice studio apartment in a respectable South Side development like Lake Meadows. Maybe they'd have been able to write it off as an understandable step toward independence. That's not what I did, though, when I left home.

I moved all the way up to the North Side, to a rambling apartment with sloping floors and niggardly steam heat, where I had anywhere from three to seven roommates, depending on who was sleeping at a lover's apartment, who was hitchhiking to California, or who was back home in Indiana for some holiday. At the moment we were without any pet critters, though it was just about time for one of our number to find another stray kitten or take in an orphaned parakeet.

Woody and Ivy Lisle are my de facto parents. My mother, Haddy Perry, left me in my grandmother's care when I was eight, and she's been in the wind ever since. The years with Grandma Perry were brief but hideous. To put it mildly, we never hit it off. And, in a masterpiece of understatement, let me say I was not a happy child.

As I get older, I try not to blame her so much for her part in my misery. The best I can figure, she and my mother had never been the greatest of pals, and as soon as Mom was of age, she cut herself loose from home and hearth. Then, at just the time in the old lady's life when child rearing should have been far behind her, she got saddled with a needy youngster—that would be me—subject to bouts of depression, panic, and rage.

Like her husband before her, Grandma was *called home,* in the Negro parlance, at a fairly young age. My guess is, she had had it up to here and was good and ready to go. At any rate, that's when her younger sister Ivy took me in.

As for my biological father? You tell me. My family history is lousy with secrets, vague explanations that don't hold water, and outright lies. The story of how I came into being partakes of every one of those things.

The three years with my weary grandmother at her house on Forest Street, at the heart of the heart of the South Side's ghetto, are now a blur of loneliness and resentment. Ivy and Woody saved me.

I was spared from the home for wayward juveniles and the welfare rolls, if not from a revolving cast of school bullies who hassled the shit out of me for being teacher's pet.

Under the fond gaze of Woody and Ivy, my love for reading and excelling at school was rewarded with gift-boxed fountain pens, season subscriptions to the Young People's Orchestra, and summers at theater arts camp, where I painted flats for *Death Takes a Holiday* and then wowed them as Berenice in *The Member of the Wedding.*

And at home I got away with murder: my own television, no

bedtime curfew, allowed to drink coffee with my breakfast and mingle with the cocktail party guests, sipping 7-Up from a martini glass and eating myself stupid on deviled shrimp canapés.

So, goody-good little Cassandra, who used to write those prize-winning essays for Negro History Week, joined a hippie commune. Yep, I'm all grown up now, twenty years old, and taking my rightful place as a black freak. With visions of group sex, drug addiction, and me never again folding my dinner napkin, my very proper aunt Ivy had near about fainted when I broke the news.

I took a big pull from the joint I was sharing with Wilton and passed it over to him—tried to, anyway. He was lost in his own thoughts now, and didn't notice me until I made a fist and knocked gently on his forehead.

Those limpid eyes of his seemed to shine love out at me.

My friend Wilton's upbringing, despite the fractured grammar he affected, had been even more rarefied than mine. Both his parents were of the black professional class, mother a pediatric surgeon and father a big-bucks attorney. Wilton was born into the high bourgeoisie, as his parents and their parents before them had been. Fact, going back to the Reconstruction, his family tree hung heavy with scientists, teachers, and industrialists.

In keeping with the cloud cover over my family history, I really don't know where my aunt Ivy's refinement or my uncle Woody's money came from.

I was grateful to Woody and Ivy for converting my life from shit to sugar. I tried never to hurt or disappoint them, and I'd been the best girl I could be for a long time.

If you asked them, they'd likely say my days as an obedient child had ended without notice some time during the month of April 1968. I guess they'd be right. Something had happened to me that record-setting, murderous spring, with its weather from heaven and headlines from hell. You ticked off the horrors as spring folded into summer: King murdered; urban riots; the war inflating like a corpse in muddy water; RFK murdered; students assaulted and killed all over the globe.

And then there was the convention, Chicago's local sideshow that turned into a world event and made Richard J. Daley a bigger star than Jane Fonda.

But I had my own list of upheavals, events in my personal life that shook me down to my shoes, things that were changing me, shaping me, making me for better or worse into someone else—

—Number one, I'd been witness to an ugly murder, and very nearly a second victim. Woody's nephew had been knifed in the old neighborhood, just minutes from my grandmother's Forest Street house, and I had watched him die.

—Then, too, a beloved friend had disappeared on me, doing nothing less than altering the course of my life along with his.

—Another change revolved around loss, too, but it had nothing to do with war or death. Quite the opposite. Contrary to my long-held belief that I'd go to my grave without ever getting laid, I finally did. A fellow named Melvin had deflowered me under some pretty harrowing circumstances. But that didn't stop me from loving it.

Melvin was long gone. But openhearted, decent, handsome, ironic Wilton Mobley truly liked and understood me, wanted to be my friend. The feeling was ever so mutual. When he invited me to move in, it looked as though I'd fallen into a honeypot. It just seemed natural that Wilt and I, two Afro-American freaks, would get together, maybe even build some kind of life that would outlast our time at the commune.

My luck is strange, though. I have this giveth-and-taketh-away thing going with the gods. Wilton never became my lover. Instead he was devoted to a lissome white girl named Mia, whose complexion was something out of a Vermeer and whose disposition and heart were so lovely, you almost expected to see sparrows tweeting in formation around her head. Mia Boone was the mothering, pie-baking, herb-gardening, homemade-soap, meat's-no-good-for-you, mantra-chanting, candle-burning heart of the commune, and she and Wilton were so much in love it made me feel dirty to imagine either of them with another partner.

As I was doing most days as of late, I had blown off my classes, telling myself I'd read like crazy long into the night and be caught up with everything by the end of the week. And for the nonce, I was whiling away the afternoon with Wilton, smoking his excellent weed. The new heater was doing its thing and we were doing ours.

Then, through my laughter, I heard Mia call from the kitchen, "Lunch, guys!"

At the sound of her voice, Wilton's ears pricked up like a devoted Great Dane hearing his master's step on the gravel path.

"You better get a move on, Wretched, or there won't be any delicious vegetarian tacos left," I said.

I started calling him Wretched because it was taking him so goddamn long to finish reading Fanon's book. The dog-eared paperback had been gathering dust on the TV table for months. After a while, he began calling me Wretched, too. It was a bit of conspiratorial silliness. But I took a childish thrill in the easy, telegraphic way Wilt and I communicated. I knew it probably made the others feel excluded sometimes. And I knew it wasn't worthy of me. But it was fun.

I heard a child's voice out in the hallway, too. It belonged to little Jordan. Who rarely missed a meal at our place. The ten-year-old son of a junkie couple up the block, he spent the bulk of his time in our apartment. In the journal I was keeping the first few weeks I lived here, I referred to him as the feral boy. That sounds snotty and heartless. I didn't mean it that way at all. I actually kind of like the boy, and God knows I feel sorry for him. But until I got to know him a little better, I was almost afraid he would bite me if I approached him. That's how bizarre he was.

Jordan had attached himself to Mia because she was the source of food. He bonded with Cliff Tobin, another commune resident, because Cliff was so generous with his time, attention, and empathy. He bought roller skates and ice cream cones for the kid, watched over him as he slept on the cot in Cliff's room, took him hiking, taught him how to swim, and generally placed himself between Jordan and the nasty realities of the boy's parents' life. In return, Jordan stood ready to lay down his little life for his ultimate big brother. Understandable. In his place, I'd have done the same.

I heard dishes clanging dimly in the massive kitchen, conversation, laughter. I remained where I was, on the makeshift hearth before the heater. I was thinking back on the weekend we'd all spent at the Wisconsin farmhouse owned by the parents of one of our roommates, Annabeth Riegel.

Oh, we had a great time on those enchanted walks in our clunky boots through the muddy fields, tripping like mad on the acid one of our number had supplied. And we had gorged on Mia's gingerbread and mountains of her hand-churned ice cream. But I remembered feeling weird as I stood alone watching the sun rise from the attic window. Not lonely. Not envious of the ones who were coupling downstairs. Just a bit ill at ease.

"Sandy?"

I looked up. Cliff was in the doorway.

That's right, he'd called me Sandy. Everyone in the house did. Not Cass—by which I had been known all my life until I packed my suitcases and moved to Armitage Avenue—Sandy.

I loved being called that.

"Great tacos," Cliff said. "Better hurry up."

"Okay. I'm coming."

Another male voice rang out then. "*You're coming!* Close the door, for Christ's sake."

That master wit was Barry Mayhew, an on-again, off-again

roommate fifteen years or so older than any of the rest of us. I
didn't know the full story on him, only that he had had some kind
of white-middle-class epiphany the previous year. He'd walked
away from his straight job. Walked away from a wife and family
out in the suburbs, too. What was the mantra? Turn on, tune in,
drop out.

For Barry, the Summer of Love apparently stretched on
through the fall and winter of '67 and was still going strong at the
end of '68. His mission in life was to bed as many young women
as he could. He'd hook up with one girl or another, maybe move
in with her for a week or two. But eventually he always came
back to the commune.

As for the *turning on* part of that advice, Barry was real serious about that. Not only did he buy, sell, and smoke googobs of
dope, he was the source of some of our most memorable tabs. It
went a long way toward compensating for all the communal du-
ties he neglected—buying paper goods, swabbing the bathroom,
and so on. Barry was rarely around to do his part. But given what
he contributed over and above his share of the rent, we let him
slide.

He was at the stove now, dipping a hunk of seven-grain bread
into the cast-iron cauldron, being careful of the leather coat he
was so proud of. "Hey, Mia. You make this?"

"Yeah," she said. "Jesus, Barry, are you speeding again? It's
mealtime, okay? You're ruining the vibe."

"I'm sorry, Madam Krishna. I'll be good. But I'm serious,
baby. You can really burn some groceries."

Wilton rolled his eyes. "Be careful there, dude," he said.
"Don't spill nothing on your love beads." It was okay for Wilton
to pepper his language with underclass Negro slang, but he resented it when Barry talked that way.

On at least one occasion, Barry and Wilt had nearly come to
blows over the black language thing. Barry had used a word that

sent Wilton over the moon. He said he'd bought some bootleg records off a *spook* he knew.

Wilton was in Barry's face within a nanosecond.

"Take it easy, brother man . . . *Damn*. We supposed to be about peace and love." Barry's nervous smile reminded me of the cowardly, wisecracking persona that Bob Hope took on in those silly movies of his.

"For the last time," Wilton said, "you ain't no nigger, Barry. You haven't even earned the right to call me brother. What the fuck do you know about us? You were born and raised here, but you don't know shit about what the South Side of Chicago means. Look at somebody like Cliff—old Yankee Connecticut and shit, man. Ask him who Gwendolyn Brooks is. He knows, okay? Ask him who Toussaint was, or Henry Tanner. His mother and big brother went to Selma with Dr. King, man."

"Not exactly," Cliff said meekly. "They heard him speak in Washington."

But Barry and Wilt's difficulties didn't end there. If Wilton's version of the facts was to be trusted, Barry had been after Mia from the first day he laid eyes on her. Not hard to believe. Most guys were drawn to her. It seems he and Wilt had been tossing zingers at each other ever since.

"Who's up for a function at the junction tonight?" Barry asked no one in particular. "You people are so lame," he said when no one answered.

He passed behind my chair and gave a tug to my braid. "What's happening, Sandy? You want to party with me, don't you, you little sex goddess?"

He was making fun of me. Barry never ceased hitting on Mia. He flirted with our roommate Annabeth Riegel, too, and with Clea, a black friend of hers who was at the apartment often enough to be considered a roommate. But never once had he shown any interest in me.

"Sandy's out of your league, man."

It was Cliff who had spoken.

Barry bristled. "Say what?"

"She's way too smart for you," Cliff said.

Wilt leaned across the table to give him five. "Who ain't?"

They all laughed, even Barry. "That's okay," he said, "I forgive youse. Here. Here's some shit I brought you all. 'Cause I'm such a good king. You're gonna miss me when I'm gone."

He threw an overstuffed plastic Baggie at the table. The "shit" was stemless, pristine, and the color of straw. I got a buzz just from looking at it.

Barry was grinning at us.

"We'll kiss your ring some other time," Wilton said.

"Fuckin' A, you will," said Barry.

I wasn't joining in the laughter. And I wasn't really hungry, either. Suddenly restless, I soon left the table. In my room I threw a few things into my knapsack. Then I pushed into my stained brown boots and peacoat, and headed out.

②

GRAY SNOW WAS FLUNG THIGH HIGH AGAINST THE PARKED automobiles. The neighborhood porches and front yards were festooned with Christmas tree lights and those dumb plastic Santas. I bet Forest Street, in the haunted neighborhood where I'd lived with Grandma, looked this way, too, even though it was miles away, almost in another world. Ole Chicagotown was the most rigidly segregated city in the nation, but at Christmastime most neighborhoods, black or white, tended to look the same: gaudy and sad. I wondered if it was that way all over the world.

Well, probably not in London. I bet Christmastime London was a tasteful wonderland of gaslit Victorian froufrou. That particular city was in and out of my thoughts a lot these days. I'd been a front-runner for a fellowship that would have taken me to England to study for a year. But I had pretty much blown that. So much for figgy pudding, whatever that was. For a while now, my studies have been limited to the fine distinctions between Panama Red and Acapulco Gold.

Feeling the wrath of the wind, I quickened my pace. When I reached North Avenue, I turned into the little cul-de-sac of Vine Street. My guy, Nat Joffrey, wouldn't be home yet, but I had the key to his place, the ground-floor apartment in a rickety two-flat that had probably been built about 1850, not unlike the pitiful housing thrown up around that time in another part of town to house the stockyard workers.

Nat was one of the better people in the world. A Negro born and raised on the North Side, he was part troubadour, part philosopher, part oracle. He had a wonderful baritone voice that made him a charismatic speaker at rallies.

Kindhearted Nat, when he wasn't bagging granola and hosing down organic celery at the Food Coop, worked tirelessly for the peace movement, edited and published political broadsides, organized folk music festivals, volunteered at skid row soup kitchens. The list went on. He was fifty-one, more than thirty years my senior. He was also beginning to lose his woolly hair, and he had a body as formless as a sack of baking potatoes and a face just this side of homely. In other words, every bit of his beauty was on the inside.

Naturally, he was madly in love with me.

When he arrived, he was loaded down with groceries. Trying to help him, I reached for a couple of the earth-friendly Food Coop bags. He wouldn't let me take them, though. All he wanted to do was kiss me. Grapefruits and lentils and unshelled peanuts went all over the floor while we stood there going at it. Five minutes later, we hit the bedroom.

Seeing me shiver, he struck a wood match for the gas heater. "You go to school today?"

Instead of answering, I sighed.

"Uh-huh. What'd you do all day? Hang around and smoke grass?"

"More or less."

"What are your folks going to say if you flunk out?"

"I'm not going to flunk out, Nat."

"You will if you keep on hanging around with Wilton and them."

"Right. We ought to be more productive members of society. And if I moved in here and had you nagging me all the time, I would be."

He smiled in his ragged way; tooth broken in a fight during his stint in the segregated WWII army and never repaired. "You'd think that spoiled brat could find something better to put his mind to than staying high."

"I know, Nat. He's just not your favorite pothead."

"He's spoiled, I tell you. Lazy. Directionless. Talking that shit about offing the pigs . . . being militant. Huh. I'd like to see him handle it in the goddamn military, the way they drafting all these penniless, half-ignorant black boys and sticking them on the front lines over there."

"In case you don't remember, Nat, we're supposed to be *against* the military. Wilt doesn't want to see anybody drafted and stuck on the front lines."

He was in his anti-Wilton groove now, unstoppable. "And if there's anybody in the world got less business owning a gun, I'd like to know who."

I rolled my eyes. The gun thing was complicated. Even I thought it was a mistake for Wilt to have one. But he had bought it for protection, he said. There had recently been break-ins all over the neighborhood. As the rumor mill had it, gangs of white thugs had been raiding so-called hippie pads, ripping off whatever drugs were around, beating up on the guys, raping the girls.

"I told you," I said, "he got rid of that thing. Mia made him. She said she wouldn't live with a gun in the house."

"Bad as things are for niggers in this city, there's a hundred other things he could be doing," Nat grumbled.

"There're things we could be doing, too," I said, hoping it would shut him up. "Why don't you put down that bag of brown rice. I didn't come over to talk about Wilt. I came to see you, didn't I?"

Yes, I realized, that's why I had left the lunch table. I'd suddenly felt in need of erotic comforting. Maybe it was Barry's teasing that had set me off. I didn't know. I just knew I wanted to be with someone who didn't take my sexuality as a joke.

Nat had that same faintly acrid odor about him as my very first lover. There was salt in it, and unsweetened cocoa. He was careful with me, too, the way Melvin had been. I liked being caressed in that delicate way and I liked all those kisses. But I wasn't a virgin anymore; I was hungrier, bolder, and I wanted more. I wanted something I couldn't name yet, or even imagine. And I could never quite help wondering how different it would be with a guy like Wilton, whose body was sleek and quick and who had been with so many other lovers. Wouldn't I be utterly spent and out of my head with pleasure now if that were Wilton smiling down at me, rolling onto the other pillow?

WILT HAD A RUDE NICKNAME FOR MY LOVER—HE CALLED him *De Lawd*—taken from some creepy old musical about Negroes in heaven. I felt really guilty for laughing at Nat behind his back. But, laugh I did.

Men. And their little jealousies. And their little hypocrisies. I wanted to understand them, not just sexually, but in all their confounding complexity. I didn't, yet. Some women just get them right off the bat, instinctively. But women like that are always slinky. Which I certainly wasn't. However, right after the holidays, I was going to lose fifteen pounds. I want to be an established slinky by the time I'm twenty-one.

CHAPTER TWO
TUESDAY

Nat woke me at 6 fucking a.m., and then made me eat oatmeal, the pebbly kind, from Ireland. After that, we walked to the corner together.

"I don't have any classes today," I assured him. "I mean, even if I wanted to go, I don't have classes on Tuesday. Honest."

He gave me a good-bye kiss on the forehead. Then he headed off for the el station, and I started walking back to Armitage.

The weather was a little milder that morning. We'd had no overnight snowfall, for a change. It was my turn to buy paper goods for the house. I did the shopping at the Jewel, and before I headed home I indulged in a couple of doughnuts at the Dairy Queen on Clark Street.

Barely 10 a.m., but the apartment was raucous when I arrived with my packages. Beth and Clea Benjamin, her friend and co-worker at the boutique on Lincoln Avenue, were dancing deliriously in the front room, warbling all out of tune with the Supremes.

"Sandy!" Annabeth called out. "We got the place."

The place? What did she mean?

Oh, right. The *place*—upstairs. Our communal apartment was roomy by most standards. Still, we were beginning to trip over one another. Beth had come from money. Her parents didn't much like the life she was living, and they kept threatening to cut off her allowance. But so far, those whopper checks were still a monthly cause for celebration. Beth had got wind of a vacancy on the floor above. "Far out!" she kept saying. "We're going to have a fucking freak duplex. Upstairs and down. It's gonna be great, guys."

"The place, Sandy. You wanna move up or stay down here?"

"I don't know," I said. "I guess it depends."

Clea stopped spinning, turned her nose up at me. "Depends on whether Wilton and *her* move up. You do whatever they do, right?" *Her*—as far as Clea was concerned, Mia didn't have an actual name—just *her*.

Clea was small and pretty, with a beautiful figure. But I swear I don't know why Annabeth liked her. Clea could be so mean. It was unfortunate that she didn't like me much, either. I had tried to make friends with her, but to no avail. I was just happy she didn't officially live at the commune.

The way I saw it, Clea was attracted to Wilton but the feeling wasn't mutual. Which must have stung her. She had had tons of boyfriends, I was told, and was accustomed to getting anybody she wanted. So her resentment of Mia was threefold: Mia had a man Clea felt ought to be hers, Mia was white and had a man Clea felt ought to be hers, and Mia was white and had a black man Clea felt ought to be hers.

As to why she disliked me, I figured there was something old and visceral about her antagonism, probably dating back to her childhood, and mine: I was the kind of kid who drew the wrath of her kind of kid like iron filings to a horseshoe.

I went to my room and tossed my bag on the bed. On the bureau was a beribboned chocolate Santa Claus propped up against my bottle of hand lotion.

"It's from Jordan and me," Cliff said, suddenly at my shoulder.

"Thanks. How come I rate this? It's not Christmas yet."

Couldn't hear his answer. Shy Cliff tended to mumble when he was embarrassed. I broke off a foot and handed it to him, popped the other one into my mouth.

"So what do you think?" he asked. "You want to move up to the new place or stay here?"

"I'm not sure. I'm just glad we're getting some more space."

"Yeah. Beth's picking up most of the new rent, but if Clea moves in, it'll be even cheaper."

Clea?

There it was again. Giveth and taketh away.

"Is Clea moving in?"

"She's thinking about it."

Shit, shit, shit.

Nobody was invited to move in unless the whole group agreed. We all ate together, did chores together, watched TV together. I'd be living with somebody constantly bad vibing or patronizing me. The thought of it was hideous. No, I'd have to turn thumbs down on her. But if I blackballed Clea, then Annabeth would be mad at me.

Of course, there was another option: I could leave. It made me sick to think about it, but I just might have to be the one to leave.

I started picking through the ashtray, looking for a roach. "Does Wilt know she might move in?" I asked.

He shrugged.

"Where is he, anyway? Him and Mia."

"I don't know. Haven't seen them since lunch yesterday. I figured they told you where they were going."

"No. You mean they didn't sleep here last night?"

"Uh-uh."

Taylor Simon, Wilton's buddy from Antioch, had come into
the room by then. He was on the short side, well-muscled, with
an infectious grin. He and I often played Scrabble to the death.

"Who didn't sleep here last night?" Taylor asked. Between a
new girlfriend and the job he had at *Rising Tide,* an alternative
magazine that had started up last year, we hadn't seen much of
him lately.

"Mia and Wilt," I said. "Where could they be?"

"Maybe Mom and Dad needed a break from us kids. I guess
they could've gone with Dan on one of his psilocybin vacations in
the forest primeval. They'll all come home tripped out and
smelling bad. Anyway, boys and girls, get your filthy clothes together. Me and Cliff have laundromat duty, and then I gotta get
to work."

I closed my door and lit up as soon as they left.

Bay-bay, everything is all right. Uptight! Out of sight.

Beth and Clea's little record hop was even louder now. I could
still hear their merriment. I thought sourly, the only thing I have
to celebrate is finding the butt of this abandoned joint.

At the same moment I realized I'd left my book at Nat's place,
the Hawthorne I was supposed to be reading for American Lit, I
heard a dull thud above my head. Funny, but I could also have
sworn I heard an agonized moan. Double funny—the apartment
upstairs was vacant. It was going to be the upper floor of our duplex.

I opened my door and looked out to see Clea and Annabeth
rushing out of the apartment. They were headed upstairs. I followed.

A bucket of soapy water was overturned on the landing. Mr.

Fish, the building superintendent, lay writhing in the doorway of the empty apartment, his mop clutched in his hand.

Annabeth leaned down to pry the mop handle from his fingers. Must be a heart attack. "Get an ambulance, Sandy!"

I was headed back down to our place when I heard another scream—Clea's. I knew instantly she wasn't wailing in grief over Mr. Fish. There was too much terror in that cry. I ran back up and shoved her aside.

Oh, Lord. There was every reason to think that old man's heart had exploded when he caught sight of this. Mia was face-down on the floor of the deserted apartment, dark blood clotting her hair. She was wearing her sweet white wool jumper with the embroidery around the neck and hem, tiny Dutch children in their wooden shoes.

Across the room, Wilton was anchored with rope to a folding chair, eyes bugged, throat slit, his shirtfront soppy and black. Hard as I tried, I couldn't turn away.

I was standing in Mia's blood. Her life all liquid under the soles of my boots. But I couldn't move, couldn't turn away from the stiff and swollen torso in that old chair. That thing turning to rancid meat had been my friend Wilton, who always had a joke for me, and whose quick mind and kind heart had been my delight in living. Soul brother. An expression I never used. But that was what he had been. How could I turn away?

Uptight! Out of sight! said Stevie. I couldn't hear what Beth was shouting, but I heard Little Stevie.

"Shut up," I cried.

And if I couldn't turn away now, couldn't literally go, then I'd just have to escape to some other place in my own head.

So I did that. I went somewhere else. I went back to the park, and I was there with Wilt.

2

THAT CONVENTION WAS THE DAMNEDEST THING. FROM JANUARY through July, the pileup of terrible events was staggering, more evil than we ever dreamed we could endure. But then the Democrats came to town, and the violence turned psychedelic.

It was bedlam in the Civic Center. Mayor Daley was really showing his ass, venting his murderous, red-faced rage. Ah, but there was a place where things were different, a spot where, as Mia might say, the vibe was mellow. Lincoln Park was drawing young people like so many ants to an abandoned wedding cake. I was no exception. I heard the music of youth all the way on the other side of town, and every day I'd climb on the Michigan Avenue bus to make the long trip north, not returning to Hyde Park until the small hours.

Woody and Ivy questioned me about how I was spending my days. My answers were always polite, containing next to no solid information. The less they knew, the better.

I had read somewhere that Bobby Seale and Jean Genet would be speaking in the park. I knew the former, of course, but wasn't exactly sure who the latter was. It was my friend and one-time English Lit professor, Owen Kittridge, who told me.

While I listened to Genet lecture in broken English, a tall, good-looking guy with a tangled 'fro took a seat near me on the grass. About ten minutes later, the ripsaw snoring began. The same cute, nappy-haired young man was sprawled out, dead to the world, making so much racket that Genet had to cut his speech short.

I remained there on the grass watching over the man I would soon come to know as Wilton Mobley as he slept like a baby. When he came to, an hour or so later, he rubbed his eyes very much as an infant would. "Got a smoke for me?" he asked.

And there went my heart.

We talked for hours, astonished to discover that his parents lived six blocks from Woody and Ivy in Hyde Park. But he had not lived with his folks since he'd come home from Antioch. They were furious that he'd dropped out. To escape their ire, he had taken a room in the same communal apartment on the North Side where an ex-classmate, Taylor Simon, lived.

I had found this wonderful boy in the park, a sleepyhead black prince, like something out of a fairy tale, and we agreed on everything:

What music did I listen to?

Yeah, he liked them, too.

Was I as sick of school as he was?

Pretty much.

Was I worried how I'd fit into the revolution, and was I equally as scared as I was excited?

Oh, yes . . . yes.

But had I had any of Owsley's acid?

Jesus, wasn't it amazing!

No end to the stuff we were solid on.

Some nice old white ladies making a tour of the park with a huge picnic basket gave us egg salad sandwiches and tangerines. As darkness fell, we smoked a joint together. I looked up at the stars, happy. Imagine it. Somebody like this, and eight hours ago I didn't know he existed. Friends for life now, I thought—hoped.

Wilton said he had to take a leak and went off in search of one of those portable toilets. Before he could make his way back to me, people around me began to rise in waves. A wordless panic had taken hold of the masses. Then the tear gas settled over us like a cloak. I ran for it, blind, like a baby goat separated from its mother. The marathon conversation with my new best friend would have to wait for another day.

No matter, though. We had time. I'll see him again, I told my-self. I have his number at the commune.

ON THE DAY HE FIRST TOOK ME THERE, I WAS A NERVOUS WRECK. IT *was dinnertime, so most of the crew was in residence.*

His voice was cheery as he introduced me to the others. "Hey, muthafuckahs, I got my little friend with me. All of y'all, say hello to Cassandra."

His little friend? Lord, why did he have to put it that way? Wilton was all of twenty-three.

He hung his key ring on the Shaker coat rack behind the front door and then ushered me in.

Mia left her post at the stove and came over to embrace me. She'd heard so much about me; she knew how much Wilt thought of me and hoped I would become her good friend, too.

"What do people call you—Sandy?" she asked.

"Yes," I lied.

At the table, I sat between Cliff Tobin, a lanky fellow from Connecticut who was a psych major at DePaul, and Dan Zuni, who took classes at the Art Institute. Despite his name, Mia in-formed me, he was in fact not a Zuni Indian but of the Isleta Pueblo tribe. Dan, who didn't talk a lot, smiled appreciatively at her for the explanation.

Wilton often referred to his former classmate Taylor as "the grown-up," since Taylor seemed to have already found his way in the world. He was serious about becoming a crack investigative journalist.

Annabeth Riegel, the rich girl, had once wanted to be an ar-chaeologist. But she had dropped out, like Wilton and Taylor. Now she was taking acting classes several nights a week, hoping someday she'd be accepted at the Goodman Theatre.

The one commune member not in residence that night was Barry Mayhew. Not much was said about him. In fact, there was a bit of eye-rolling at the mention of his name. But I did get the sense that his contribution to communal life was a vital one, and that it was chemical in nature.

Between the cream of celery soup that started the meal and the berry pie that ended it, I heard enough of the bits and pieces of everybody's story to kind of fit together how these people had ended up together:

Annabeth needed a head shot of herself and hired Dan Zuni, who was a gifted photographer.

Cliff arrived in town too late to get a room in the dorm, so he posted a notice at the Food Coop, where Mia just happened to be looking at a "couch for sale" sign at the same moment.

Taylor and Annabeth met at a party, got to talking about movies. He was looking for a place to live, he said. By the end of the week, he had moved in.

Wilton and Mia, strangers, were both at the 3 Penny Cinema the night it ran the underground favorite Chafed Elbows. He found the mitten she'd dropped under his seat. Their eyes met. After the movie, over bancha tea at the local health food café, they pledged their lives to each other.

One friend, one lover, one life folding into another. The freak network, as Wilton called it. "We always manage to find each other," he said. "Soon as I met Cassandra, I knew she was one of us."

After supper, Mia went off to her meditation class. I joined the others at a dingy club on Wells Street for a rare appearance by Otis Spann. We drank barrels of cheap red wine, and when the last set was over we hiked to the lot where Dan Zuni kept his wreck of a car, toking up all the way. Dan was going to drive me home, so everybody piled in and went along for the trip to Hyde Park. When Dan pulled into the driveway of the building where I lived with Uncle Woody and Aunt Ivy, I didn't want to get out of the car. I finally did, though, and waved good-bye to them all.

I couldn't sleep that night. I was too happy. Around three in the morning, I switched on the radio. That was sufficient to bring me down. Death toll for the week so far: 112. The figure sat in my mind. I began to picture them. One hundred and twelve dead American boys laid end to end. Missing limbs. Stomachs blown open. Some headless. Meat. And then there was all that enemy meat, the barefoot peasants who were kicking our ass.

I lit a cigarette, got out of bed, and walked over to the window. I searched the night for the house where Wilton's parents lived. Maybe I'd meet them some day. Maybe they'd like me and I'd be the one to broker a reconciliation between them and Wilt.

We talked about Vietnam a lot, Wilton and I. I estimated a good 50 percent of the boys from the poor school I'd attended in my grandmother's neighborhood wound up in 'Nam. Wilton figured nobody from his class at Francis Parker was there. But this brother he knew, Alvin, had been there. Alvin was outtasight. He was a real black man.

"I'm glad I'm not a man," I whispered to him. The two of us were at a teach-in, listening to this legless vet speak about the war.

"Me too," he said, and took my hand. "I'm glad you not a man, too."

③

YOU CAN'T FALL APART. THAT'S WHAT I KEPT THINKING AS I watched the cops move in and out of our rooms.

Beth and Clea had not loved Wilt like I had. But they were falling apart. Useless. So I had to take a hand in things. *I* had to call the ambulance for Mr. Fish. *I* had to call the police for Mia and Wilt. *I* had to find the phone number of the laundromat and summon Taylor and Cliff back to the house.

My cool-cucumber act must have been working. Like the uniformed cops who first showed up, the tall detective from the
homicide squad was directing all his questions to me. He was fair-
haired with pitted skin and blue eyes that seemed never to blink.
Playing the Quiet American, strong and silent. Poking into our
things, judging us. I despised him.

He opened the door to Wilt and Mia's room with a gloved
hand. "This where they slept?" he demanded.

"You never even showed your badge," I said.

"What?"

"This isn't the crime scene. This is a private home. You're supposed to show ID when you're in a person's home—not to mention a little respect."

He stared at me for a moment, as if he was thinking about
backslapping me. "My name is Norris. James Norris. Happy
now?"

I didn't answer.

"How do you know the victim?"

"Which one? There're two victims."

"The girl."

"I met her this summer. Mia was a nice person. I mean, a good
person."

He grunted. "And him? Who was he to you?"

"My friend."

"You sleeping with him?"

"No. He was with Mia."

"So what? Everybody sleeps with everybody. Isn't that the
idea? Free love."

Mia and I had been arrested a couple of months before at a
housing rally. We were thrown in the women's lockup at Cook
County Jail until Nat raised bail money. Most of our companions
in the cell were prostitutes. According to them, the Chicago cops

were no strangers to free love. I didn't point that out to Norris, though. I just said, quietly, "Wilton was my friend."

"You jealous?"

"What did you say?"

"You saying you weren't jealous? He was putting it to the white girl, wasn't he? Stud like him. He had a regular harem in here. But he wasn't putting it to you. You mean to say that didn't make you mad?"

"Somebody killed my friends. I'm pretty mad about that."

"Yeah, you're jealous all right. Why don't you tell me what happened?" He flipped out his notepad then, suddenly, brandishing it like a saber.

"I can account for every minute of my time since one o'clock yesterday."

"Save it. The other colored girl—was she having sex with him?"

"Wow. You're unbelievable. I thought they made you take some sort of intelligence test before they promoted you to detective."

He came close to laying hands on me at that. But he didn't. He ordered me out of the room.

The crowd of cops and technicians pushed us farther and farther away from the center of the apartment. Cliff and Taylor were flanking Clea, who was shaking.

There was some kind of stir about where Norris was going to set up an interrogation room. He settled on the sunporch where Taylor and Barry Mayhew slept.

"Fuck," Taylor muttered.

"What is it?" I asked.

"Barry stashes in there. What if they go snooping in his stuff?"

"Don't they have to have a warrant to do that?" Cliff asked.

"Yeah, Cliff," Taylor said. "They care a lot about that kind of thing."

Jesus. That was all we needed. Getting busted on the same day two friends get slaughtered.

"Barry's probably going to walk in here any minute," I said. "No telling what he'll do."

Taylor answered, "He'll rat us out in about two seconds, probably tell them the dope is mine."

One by one, Norris called us in. When Cliff came out of the room, he looked all caved in, on the verge of tears.

I looked away from him, willing myself to keep it together.

The cops had been in the apartment for hours. It was dark now, but when I glanced out of the window, blinding lights were shining up at me. The local news station had sent a van and equipment. The sidewalk below was alive with people. Reporters, neighbors, onlookers, medics, uniformed police.

"Oh, God, Cliff. Jordan's down there. Look."

"He must be scared out of his mind. I'm going down to get him."

He didn't, though. The cops wouldn't let him leave. Cliff stalked the living room like a crazed horse. He must have been thinking, as I was, that those junkie skanks who called themselves Jordan's parents had no business letting him roam around at night. I wished they would both overdose and let Cliff raise him.

The cops were allowing Clea to go home. As she pulled into her coat, she could barely look at me.

"You okay?" I asked.

She nodded. "I just want to get out of here."

It shamed me, but the thought did fly through my mind: not much chance I'll have to worry about her moving in now.

Annabeth was smoking furiously when they released her from the interrogation session. She turned her back to the cop who was picking through the back issues of *Rising Tide* on the coffee table and spoke low and urgently. "Where the fuck is Dan? That cop is asking all this stuff about who lives here and he sounds like he thinks Dan might have done it."

Lord. In all the confusion, I had forgotten about Dan Zuni. I looked over at Cliff, repeated the question. "Where is Dan?"

"Taking photos, I guess."

"*Where?*"

"Who knows."

It wasn't at all unusual for Dan to take off by himself for days at a time. He'd throw a few things in the back of the car and go into the woods to take photos, to think—meditate, as Mia called it—or to enjoy the peyote a friend had laid on him.

Of course, it was just as likely that he'd met some girl and gone off with her. Dan was spacy by nature, and a loner, but he had that gorgeous mane of silken hair, that burnished skin and those arresting black eyes. Females couldn't get enough of him.

The cops let us make tea. It felt weird to be puttering at the stove. The kitchen had been Mia's province. I didn't get to drink mine, though. Detective Norris had saved the best for last, so to speak. He crooked his finger at me, calling me out to the sun-porch.

Man, that guy rubbed me the wrong way. Earlier, the feeling had seemed to be mutual, and then some. But Norris's manner had softened a little by the time I took a seat across from him on the foldout sofa.

The questions he put to me about Wilt and Mia went all over the map—jealous exes, drug deals, enemies, gang membership, Mafia ties, sexual kinks, satanic cults.

I guess my answers jibed sufficiently with what the others had told him. As the interview rolled on, he even deigned to answer a couple of my questions.

"Did you take those ropes off of him? Are they gone yet? The bodies, I mean."

"Yeah. They're on the way to the morgue."

"How long were they laying there like that? You've got some kind of tests to tell you that, haven't you?"

"Hard to say. The ME's gonna have fun with this one. There's no heat in that place. It being so cold, they coulda been killed yesterday afternoon or late last night. Why do you ask?"

I shrugged. "I don't know, really."

But I did know. I was being stupidly messianic. I couldn't help thinking that if I'd stayed at home, or if I hadn't decided to spend the night at Nat's, I could somehow have stopped the slaughter.

"Are you finished with me now?"

"Almost." He leaned back in his chair, offered me a cigarette. "You go to the same school as Wilton Mobley?"

"No."

"Where do you go?"

"Debs."

He gave me a Gomer Pyle grin. "Huh. So you like them commie teachers?"

Off-the-wall question. But I knew what he meant. Debs College had been founded in the 1930s by a renegade group of Socialist academics fed up with the ivory-tower mentality and racial quotas. From all accounts, it was a glorious hotbed. But now, some thirty years later, there was little difference between it and just about any other midlevel university.

"I like them okay," I said. "They're better than fascists anyway."

As the interrogation wound down, I couldn't help thinking that I'd much rather deal with the fat-ass street cops who had busted heads in Lincoln Park than a jerk like Norris. At least you could usually outrun them.

CHAPTER THREE

WEDNESDAY

1

I LAY THERE LISTENING TO THE OTHERS IN THE KITCHEN. THE room was freezing cold. I had forgotten to put the heater on and had slept—if you could call it that—all curled up, the covers pulled over my head. I knew I had to get out of bed sooner or later, but the effort seemed enormous. This huge weight was on my chest, and my eyes were crusted over.

Finally I got up and pulled my woolen sailor pants and a warm turtleneck out of the closet. I dressed myself slowly, concentrating minutely on each task and trying to block out what had happened. Not just what had already happened, but what lay ahead: police investigations; funerals; facing not one but two sets of grieving, freaked-out parents. How were we going to get through it? How long was my little chin-up/grown-up masquerade going to last?

I didn't even bother to brush my teeth. I walked into the kitchen, the heaviness still upon me.

They were all drinking coffee, all rumpled and funky, and nobody looked any better than I did.

"We ought to go out and get a paper," Taylor was saying.

"Why?" I said acidly. "Don't you remember what happened? Wilt and Mia are dead." I knew I had no business snapping at Taylor that way. "I'm sorry," I blurted out, and along with the apology the tears erupted.

Annabeth put her arm around my shoulders, and Cliff poured coffee for me. After I was all cried out, Taylor spoke. "Well, what now?"

"For one thing, somebody's got to find Dan," said Annabeth. "The cops are looking for him, and the longer he's gone, the more it looks like he's running away. Barry, too."

"He's got to hear about it, right?" said Cliff. "I mean, it must be in all the papers, TV."

Taylor snorted. "I guess you forgot that Dan lives on Planet Zuni. When did you ever know him to pay any attention to the news? Besides, he's probably fifty miles from nowhere, shitting in the bushes."

I had an image of Dan then. Lying on his back, looking the way he did when he was high, mouthing the words to "Suzie Q."

All the what-ifs began to play across my mind. "What if they try to arrest him and he runs?" I said. "Will they shoot him? What if he's stoned when they find him? What if he thinks they're not real?"

"Why don't we take it easy?" Cliff quieted me. "Look, it's too cold for him to stay outdoors for long. Maybe he's visiting somebody in the country, like one of his teachers. He's gonna be okay."

At the sound of the key turning in the lock, we took a collective breath.

Not Dan.

It was Barry Mayhew. Red-eyed, his goatee scraggly, shaking with rage. Hands down, he looked worse than any of us.

"Get me something!" he exploded.

I pushed my coffee cup toward him, but he swept it off the table. "Get me something to fucking smoke!"

Taylor made a beeline for the stash.

Barry threw himself into a chair. "Fucking motherfuckers, man. I was walking home last night, minding my own business. Next thing I know, pigs everywhere. They put me in a *car*, man. Like I'm some street trash. Some *crim*inal, man. Morons had me at the pig station since two o'clock this morning. Talking about murder. They said Wilton and Mia—oh, man. What the fuck happened here?"

Barry was still a mess, but his face began to relax as he smoked. Before long, he was narrating his harrowing experience with the true storyteller's gusto, the center of attention, all of us in a circle around him.

He'd been at an all-night party on Wacker Drive—some rich people he sold acid to—fucking straights, man—when the cops called them to check out his alibi, at first they were too scared to say he had been there—who did the pigs think they were dealing with? some dumb, stoned-out hippie?—he knew a lawyer who'd make them look like clowns—fucking A, they had to release him, or else he was gonna get fucking Kunstler on their asses—*And what the fuck is the matter with the phone, man?*

"What phone?" Annabeth said.

"I tried to call you assholes a hundred times. The line's all fucked up."

I picked up the receiver of the wall phone. Sure enough, it was dead. I went into the living room, looked at the extension in there. It was off the hook. It must have been knocked over during the chaos of last night. I replaced the receiver on the set.

When I got back to the kitchen Barry was passing joints around, still talking. "I gotta find someplace to crash," he was saying.

"What do you mean, 'someplace to crash'? You're splitting?" Taylor asked.

"Damn right. You think I'm gonna stay here and get greased like they did?"

We fell silent for a moment, partly out of embarrassment at Barry's insensitivity. But there was another element to the stunned silence. Shocking as the murders were, it hadn't even occurred to me to fear for my own safety. It was not until Barry's crude comment that I tuned in to fear.

And clearly I wasn't alone in this. I could read it on their paralyzed faces—Beth's, Cliff's, Taylor's. *Jesus Christ,* they were all thinking. *Somebody just walked into our building and murdered two people. We're not safe here.* Talk about dumb, stoned-out hippies.

I had an even worse thought then, something I bet hadn't even occurred to the others—yet. If somebody was out to get us, maybe Mia and Wilt hadn't really been the first victims. Maybe Dan Zuni had already been got. Could be he'd never made it into the woods or wherever he was headed. I didn't even dare voice that fear. We were already freaked enough.

It had been barely sixty seconds since I'd righted the telephone. Now it was ringing. Cliff picked up the kitchen extension, listened for a few seconds, then hung up.

"Who was that?" Annabeth asked.

"Some guy from the *Sun-Times.*"

"Take it off the hook again," she said.

Oh, sure. A reporter after the inside story of the scandalous hippie murders. Look what'll happen if you let your children become free-love dope freaks.

"Hey, Sandy," Cliff said, holding on to me. "You okay? You look weird."

"I'm just so cold."

"Yeah, man, it's freezing in here," Barry said. "And I'm so hungry I could eat lint. Damn, I wish—" At least he had the decency not to finish that sentence. *I wish Mia was here.* That's what he was about to say. How about some scrambled eggs, Mia? Wait a minute . . . oh, yeah, right. She's dead. "What? Don't look at me like that. What are we supposed to do?" he said. "Starve?" He popped up from the chair and rubbed his hands. "Let's go get some grub. We'll go to Chester's. I'm buying, as usual."

"I guess he's right," Annabeth said. "It feels like I haven't had anything to eat in two weeks."

We milled around stupidly, suddenly loath to lose sight of one another. It seemed to take forever to find our coats and scarves. Then, when I opened the front door, the real chill set in. I saw four angry eyes rolling around in their sockets. A black fist poised to knock on the door. It was all I could do not to scream. Facing me were my aunt and uncle.

②

MY AUNT IVY IS WHAT SOME PEOPLE WOULD CALL PRIM. SHE is a small woman with a lovely, willowy figure. It *was* willowy, anyway, before she was hospitalized earlier in the year, and nearly died. Now she is just plain skinny. But the superpale complexion and the sunken cheeks and perfect red lips suit her, too. Closing in on sixty and in poor health, she is still a beautiful woman. Nor did the illness take anything away from her impeccable manners and her modulated way of speaking.

"Damn you, Cassandra, I don't know whether to kiss you or beat the living shit out of you."

That was not the way Ivy usually talked.

"Do you know what you put us through, child? Waking up this morning and hearing about this disaster on the radio. I said, 'Woody, have mercy, Jesus, isn't that the address where Cass is?' And then when we called and called and couldn't get an answer on the telephone—Lord, Cass. The police are circling like flies downstairs. I thought you were—Do you know what we've been through? Answer me!"

But I couldn't, because Woody started in with his own version of Do You Know What We've Been Through. It was full of threats and ultimatums, and it rang through the corridor like the voice of God in a bad mood.

I had always suspected that my self-made, self-educated uncle Woody was attached to the numbers racket in his youth. My grandma only dropped hints about the shrouded past of her sister's dapper husband Woody Lisle: Maybe he was a rumrunner and maybe he was a gambler; maybe he was once the "business partner" of the notorious South Side criminal Henry Waddell. But with him standing in the doorway like that, booming at me in that commanding, whiskey-lined voice, I felt like a nickel-and-dime gambler who had welched on a debt and was ignorant enough to think he could get away with it.

"You march back into this goddamn apartment and pack your goddamn bags, young miss," was the way Woody's tirade ended.

I opened my mouth, but no words came out. I simply held my face in my hands.

"I guess this is your family, huh, Sandy?" Cliff asked.

I began to giggle insanely.

When I recovered, I asked them in. Ivy's manners won out, after all. She was coolly gracious as I introduced her to all my roommates. Woody, on the other hand, was barely civil as he looked at one after another of my rumpled friends. His long, thin frame remained tight almost to the point of snapping.

I was finally able to put a few rational words together. "We're all hungry. Nobody's had anything to eat."

"You what?" Ivy fell back into outrage. "You mean between the five of you, you can't manage to put any food on the table?"

"No, no. I don't mean it like that. It's—never mind. Please, just sit down a minute. Will you please?"

I settled my aunt and uncle in the front room and told the others to go on without me. "That your old man?" Barry asked on his way out.

"More or less."

"That old dude is clean. I love those kicks he's wearing."

I hadn't noticed Woody's shoes. But then, I didn't need to. I knew he was always shod in something English. He polished them every night before going to sleep. Like it was some kind of manic ritual for him.

From the hall, I watched Woody and Ivy for a few minutes before joining them. I could see, mixed in with their fear and anger, their distaste at the messiness of the room. This sure wasn't how I had envisioned their first visit. A far cry from me serving them sherry and Mia's almond cookies and introducing my buddy Wilton to them. I took a long breath and then walked in. "Don't say anything," I announced, startling the hell out of them.

"Cassandra—" Woody began.

"Don't say anything," I bellowed. "I'm not leaving here until they find out who killed Wilton and Mia. I'm not ditching on my friends. And I am not going back with you."

"You most certainly are," my aunt said.

"No, Ivy. No way."

She placed a restraining hand on Woody's thigh. He was about to spring up at me.

"Look," I said. "You don't understand. Wilton meant the world to me."

"Cass," she said, "why wouldn't we understand that? You mean the world to us."

"This is different."

"You mean you were living with that man," Woody said petulantly.

"Yes. No. I mean, I loved him in a different way. Kind of the way I feel about the other people who live here, only stronger."

"Not stronger than you love your family, Cassandra," he said. "You don't love strangers more than your family."

I tried to choose my words carefully. "Okay. You're right. In a way. But I can feel close to other people—strangers, if that's what you want to call them—in a way I can't feel close to family. They just get things that you don't. We're all going through the same stuff."

"Cass, no one is saying you can't keep these people as friends. But that doesn't mean you have to live in the same house with them," Ivy said. "You can feel just as strongly about . . . these people . . . living at home."

"I am at home, Ivy."

"No, you aren't, honey."

"You're not getting it, are you? I moved out of your home. This is my home."

"There's been some killing done in your precious home," Woody shouted. "You had a safe place to live with us, girl—with your own. Everything you needed. But you had to run off to be with these people. You're not like these white youngsters, Cassandra. They got the way paved for them from the day they were born, and they still live this foolish kind of life. Now just look what it got them. You must be out of your mind to stay here after somebody's been murdered."

"Goddammit, stop calling him 'somebody.' He had a name."

He stood then, spent a few seconds attending to the crease in his trousers. Then he fixed me with one of his terrifying looks. "Cassandra, I have had just about enough of this nonsense. Get your bags."

I guess the totality of the thing had finally undone me. I was only 50 percent coherent when I started shrieking at them.

"You are driving me crazy. Suffocating me. You're fucking tyrants, both of you. You don't respect me, you don't listen to me, and you don't love me unless I do what you say. Where's that at, huh? You think you're the police? Is that it? You think I care about your bullshit neighborhood association and your corrupt Uncle Tom friends? I hate them and I hate the stupid way you live."

"Get your things, gal."

"You go to hell, Woody. I'm not going anywhere until I see some kind of justice done for Wilt and Mia. Just leave me the fuck alone."

The gallant Woody Lisle bent to help his lady to her feet. "Cass," he said, "if you were a man, I'd try to kill you."

Then he pulled Ivy, her mouth agape, out of the apartment. She slipped around the open door like an old silk scarf.

3

MY FACE WAS HIDEOUS. I BLEW MY NOSE, SWIPED AT THE residue from that hysterical bout of crying, and tore into the fried egg sandwich that Cliff had brought back for me.

"Don't cry, Sandy. I'm staying if you are."

"Thanks."

"I just called home," he said. "My mom's acting just like your people." He held a big Dixie cup full of chocolate milkshake for me to drink through the straw. "Taylor says the police wouldn't let me go home now even if I wanted to."

"Your mother's in Connecticut, right?"

"Yeah."

"I thought Connecticut was a place for people with a lot of money. But Wilt said you're not rich. He said your mom was working class and she raised you by herself."

"She did. Well, not exactly. My brother kind of raised me, too."

"You liked him a lot, didn't you?"

"Yeah, I did."

I realized too late how dumb it was of me to ask about Cliff's brother, Cary, who had been killed in Vietnam last year. Still raw from the loss, Cliff would sometimes watch the evening news coverage of the war in fascinated disgust until he could take it no more. Then he would get up and leave. Mia said a couple of times she heard him crying in his room.

Desperate to change the subject now, I asked, "Did Barry leave?"

"No. Where's he gonna go? Nobody wants him."

"Did you see Jordan?"

"Not yet. I wish I could bring him over here, but I don't think it's such a good idea."

"Yeah. Better not."

"I'm gonna go to Crash and Bev's, see if he's okay. The police have been there asking him questions."

"About us."

"Yeah. And those two assholes are mad at him for bringing heat into their house. Like the cops don't know they're idiot junkies."

Cliff continued to hold the milkshake for me, as if I were an invalid. I was sucking up the last drops when Taylor came in to tell me Nat Joffrey was on the line.

I figured Nat was worried about me. "I'm not here," I said. Making truth out of the lie, I told Cliff, "I'm coming with you. Let's go." And I grabbed my bag and coat.

I hated Nat. I knew it wasn't fair, but, just for five seconds, I let myself hate him.

I snatched the front door open, frantic to get away. I can't imagine anything in the world that could have halted my forward motion other than what I spotted out of the corner of my eye. The silver peace sign that hung from the giant ring that held Wilton's keys. There it was on one of the pegs of the coatrack. I snatched it off and kept right on going.

I took the stairs two and three at a time, leaving Cliff behind.

I knew how that goddamn conversation with Nat would have gone. I'd sooner be buried alive than endure his fatherly solicitude now. No matter what kind words he might have had for me, the real message behind them would have been "I told you so." And if he'd dared suggest that Wilton somehow brought this terrible violence down on himself, I'd have gone over there and broken something over De Lawd's woolly head.

4

"JORDAN'S FATHER. WHY DO THEY CALL HIM CRASH?"

"I don't know," Cliff said. "I guess it's something he thought was cool to call himself."

"You know what?" I said. "I know they're terrible parents and Jordan would rather be with you than live with them. But he must talk to them sometimes, right?"

"Talk about what?"

"About what he sees at the commune. He's seen Barry with a lot of dope, right? Maybe he's seen him with a wad of money, too. You think he could have told Crash and Bev stuff like that?"

"They're behind what happened to Mia and Wilt? Is that what you're thinking? What—they broke in, tied up Wilt like that, tried to get him to tell them where this big wad of money was?"

"Look, Cliff. Like you're always saying, they're asshole junkies . . . end of story."

"Yeah. Okay. But they're too stupid to do anything like that. And too strung out."

"Maybe. But what if they pump the kid for information and then sell it—like snitches—to other addicts who're more to-gether than they are? Maybe they tip off people which apart-ments are easy to break into, who's holding a supply of pills or grass or whatever."

He shook his head. "I don't see it, Sandy. I don't see Jordan telling them much of anything. He's pretty cool for his age. And besides that, he barely even talks to me. Can't you see what a fucked-up kid he is?"

No point in ringing the doorbell at Crash and Bev's place. It probably hadn't worked in years. What you did was stand on the sidewalk and yell their names until one of them heard you and came to the window. The key was then tossed down in a filthy sock.

It was Jordan who threw the window up and looked down at us. His eyes were big and terrified.

Cliff hurried up the stairs. "What's the matter?" he said as soon as the boy opened the apartment door.

Bev, his mother, lay shivering on the couch, eyes way back in her head, her lips cracked and sore-looking. She was trying to talk, but only croaks came out.

"Shit," I said, "you think she overdosed?"

"I don't think so." Cliff placed his palm on her forehead. "She's sick, though. Got a real fever."

And she stinks, I thought as I pulled the stiff army blanket at the foot of the couch up around her shoulders.

"It's freezing in here," I said.

"Jordan, get some matches," Cliff ordered. "See if the space heater works, Sandy."

"I hope they paid the gas bill," I said.

I got the heat working and then found a packet of dry soup mix, not happy about rooting around in their nasty cabinets. I boiled water and brought the hot drink over to the couch.

Bev could sit up a little by then. No light in her eyes, but even in the ruin of her thin face you saw how pretty she must have been once. She sure wasn't interested in that chicken soup, but she was too weak to lift her arm and push the cup away from her lips.

I took the cup away from her mouth for a minute and was startled when she spoke. "Still trying to heal me, huh?"

I had no idea what she was talking about. She began to slide back onto the sofa cushion, eyes flickering.

"Something happen to your mom, Jordan?" Cliff asked. "How long has she been sick?"

He was standing in a corner of the room, back to the wall. All he did was shake his head.

"Where's Crash?" Cliff said.

"I don't know. He went out."

"She looks awful, Cliff," I said. "What are you going to do?"

". . . sweet girl . . . ," Bev mumbled. "Only ones who ever help us out, you and that Indian man of yours. He's fine."

Cliff and I looked at each other. "Indian. You think she's talking about Dan?"

"She must be delirious," he said. "She thinks you're Mia."

I lifted Bev's head again, which was heavy with sleep. It was then that I realized the smell coming off the blanket was not run-of-the-mill BO. I pulled the blanket away and saw the blood soaking into the couch seat.

"Call an ambulance, Cliff. She's bleeding out."

THE AMBULANCE DRIVER TOLD US BEV HAD HAD A MISCAR-riage. Malnourishment and what looked like pneumonia—to say nothing of the heroin usage—didn't exactly make for the healthiest pregnancy. By the time they were loading the stretcher into the emergency vehicle, Jordan was hysterical. When the county social services people turned up and informed Cliff they were going to keep Jordan until his father returned, Cliff went into his own set of hysterics.

Ain't grown-up life grand? Blood and death. Just the kind of thing I bargained for when I left Ivy and Woody to strike out on my own.

I got Cliff calmed down enough to go back home. But I didn't go upstairs with him. I'd had enough of my comrades for one day. And I'd had enough of bearing up and taking charge. I swear, if we'd found any heroin in that apartment, I might have taken it myself.

I ran along the avenue, zigzagging around the deadly patches of ice. Coat collar open. No hat or gloves. The cold was deep inside me now. Rattling around in there with my grief and confusion. No, I wasn't going to turn to heroin. But I did need a drink.

⑤

STRUNG WITH LIGHTS ON A LONELY CORNER OF WILLOW Street, the Tap Root was our neighborhood bar. It was an old German beer garden that brought together a hodgepodge of white pensioner drunks, folkies and blues men from other North Side bars, college kids, journalists, the aged Wobblies from the IWW hall on Lincoln Avenue, even a few tourists who had read about the landmark watering hole in their guidebooks and were maybe hoping to meet Studs Terkel.

They served the best franks and sauerkraut at the Tap Root. Wilt and I had lunched there many a time, and as we ate, he always extracted the same promise from me—"For Christ's sake don't tell Mia. I can't take another one of her raps about preservatives."

Not much of a mix of people that day. Everybody looked old. Old and lonely. I took a stool at the bar and ordered the bitter brown ale. The Louis Armstrong concert from the juke flowed into a Jo Stafford extravaganza. I wasn't unhappy to hear that old-fashioned music; there was an odd comfort in it.

Not a soul interfered with me as I downed one tankard after another. I was getting drunk and that was just fine. It was almost enough to obliterate all the memories. Please, God, no more memories just now. Not the good ones, like holding on tight to Wilt as we roared up Lincoln Avenue on a borrowed motorcycle. And surely not the newer ones, like the sight of him in that chair, or the sucking noises my boots made as I waded through Mia's blood.

"Cass."

I turned at the sound of my name, already knowing who had spoken it.

Ivy. I wanted to speak her name in return, but I was tongue-tied.

But then she took hold of my hand and looked at me, the familiar kindness in her eyes.

It slipped out then. "I'm sorry."

"Never mind that now."

"What are you doing here?"

"I'm here for you, Cass. Your friends told me I was pretty sure to find you here. Woody's got himself under control now, baby. We all acted ugly. But we're going to get past it. All right?"

I was swaying on the barstool. I straightened myself, tried to sound authoritative. "Just because I'm calmed down doesn't mean I've changed my mind. You can't just boss me around anymore."

"Fine. Now, you lay that drink aside and let's get down to business."

I frowned at her. What business?

"Did you mean what you said about finding out who killed your friend?"

"Of course I did."

"And the rest of it?"

"What rest?"

"You said you would be willing to come back home after the killings were solved."

"I did?"

"Not in so many words. But you said you'd consider it."

"I did?"

"By implication, Cassandra."

I couldn't help it; I actually laughed.

"Well?" she said. "Are you willing to make a bargain with us? Can we come to an understanding? After justice is done, you'll give up living with—"

"With *these people,* right?"

"Cassandra, what are you laughing about?"

"Justice," I said. And then I burped.

"Are you listening to me, girl?"

"Yes, ma'am."

"Woody wants your word that you'll think about coming home after you find out what happened to your friend."

"Sure. Okay. And what's Woody's part of the bargain?"

"He's going to help you do it."

"Ain't no justice. Ain't no truth and beauty, neither," Wilton said. *May have been right here in this bar that he said it.* "Sandy, if we could learn to accept that, we'd probably be much happier Negroes."

CHAPTER FOUR

THURSDAY

MY ROOM WAS GRAY AND MUSTY FROM CIGARETTE SMOKE. IT was long past sunrise, but light was hard to come by. The news issuing from my clock radio was just as sunless and heavy—

Death toll for the week so far: 80. That was just "our" side. No figures on how many of the enemy incinerated. A Christmas truce was in the offing, and Bob Hope was on the way to Saigon.

Other headlines: Two children and their welfare mother asphyxiated. Mix poor people with no heat and a faulty gas oven. Result, death. A drunk driver killed four teens on the highway. And, near the insular working-class area where Mayor Daley was born and resided to this day, a twenty-eight-year-old black man identified as Larry Dean was found shot to death. Police said they had no leads as yet in the case.

Well, that set the right funereal tone for the day.

I moved around quietly, trying not to wake anyone. But before I left the apartment, I went in carefully to look in on them all as they slept—Taylor and Barry, Beth, Cliff. I even tipped into Dan's room, hoping against hope I'd see his lovely hair splayed across the pillow on his mat. Pretend time. I let myself fantasize for a moment. If only I could be the Good Witch, a chubby little fairy in gossamer, I'd just wave my magic wand and make all the awful shit that had marked the last two days go away. I'd even let skanky Bev keep her baby.

I WAS LUCKY TO GET A SEAT. MOST PEOPLE ON THE NUMBER 11 bus were going to work, and didn't look particularly happy about it. I didn't blame them. Who wanted to stoke the fires of capitalism taking shorthand or delivering interoffice mail in some airless coop in the Loop?

However, I was going somewhere every bit as odious. Woody had arranged for me to talk to his cop buddy, Jack Klaus, who might be able to give me the inside track on the homicide investigation. Klaus might prove to be a good source, but I didn't much like him. As the bus jerked along, I stared out the window.

Where the fuck is Dan? as Annabeth had so trenchantly put it.

Good question.

Funny about memory. I kept harking back to that stoned-out weekend we'd spent at Annabeth's family's farm in Wisconsin, how beautiful it was, how close I felt to the others, what fun we had.

So why was I constantly flashing on some out-of-place feelings from that weekend? Now I had to wonder if Dan Zuni had given off some hint of trouble then. I couldn't think of anything particularly weird about the way Dan was acting that weekend. Nothing bad had happened, or had it? Maybe the delightful mind-expanding trips I'd been enjoying were killing off brain cells quicker than you could say "Light my fire."

I MADE A BIG BOWL OF POPCORN AND TOOK IT INTO THE MUSTY SIT-ting room in the farmhouse. I was planning to leaf through some old magazines, maybe read the copy of The Marble Faun *I'd spotted on the bookshelf in there. But I was startled when Dan popped up from the sofa.*

"Oh! I didn't know you were in here. Would you rather be alone?"

He grinned at me. "No way. Come on in. Let's rap."

It cracked me up when Dan used words like rap.

"Is that popcorn?"

"Yeah. I just made it."

"Far out. I'm dying for popcorn. And look—we got beer."

"Are you stoned, Dan?"

"Uh-huh. You?"

"Yeah."

We polished off the bowl of popcorn in quick order. A few minutes later I thought I heard him humming under his breath, and he was keeping a kind of tom-tom beat on the arm of the couch.

"What's that you're singing? Creedence again?"

"No. Remember that hokey song—'Running Bear'?"

That was a blast from childhood. "Yeah. Running Bear and Little White Dove." AM radio Top Ten stuff. "They were like the Indian Romeo and Juliet. And they committed suicide at the end of the song."

He chuckled. "My pop had this big job at the BIA. Big fucking bureaucrat job. Sent me and my brother to this tight-assed private school in Tucson. The white kids used to call me Running Bear. Jesus, they were so ignorant. I thought it was funny. But Bobby, my brother, couldn't take that kind of shit. Wasn't just those kids, though. He couldn't deal with much of anything. He was always begging Pop to let us come home."

"And did he?"

Dan shook his head. "Well, he did finally. But it was too late."

"What do you mean?"

"Bobby killed himself. After that, he let us come home."

"God, Dan. I never knew that about you."

"Yep. Old Bobby. We used to talk about running away to New York. That woulda been funny."

Dan joined me on the floor then. He rolled a joint, slowly and meticulously, and let me take the first hit.

"Wilt said you and your father don't speak anymore."

He nodded. "Right. Wilt and me kind of have a lot in common. I guess we've all got bad family stuff to deal with. Like Cliff's brother getting killed. You've got a fucked-up relationship with your parents, too, don't you?"

"I don't know about fucked-up. It's not even fucked-up. I don't know where they are. I was raised by my grandmother's sister and her husband. They're older, but they're really cool."

"Me too. I mean, my grandfather took me because of all the trouble between me and my father. He's great. It's kind of great being around some old people. Except he's always after me to do my kiva ceremony."

"What's that?"

"You gotta go into a cave, pray and dance and do all kinds of shit. He says I won't really be a man until I do it."

"Are you going to do it someday?"

He shrugged. "I guess."

We smoked quietly for a few minutes until I got a little giggly. "This grass is pretty great. Where'd it come from—Barry?"

"Yeah, the Great White Father of Weed."

"Barry Running Dog," I said.

"Yeah, Barry Howling Wolf."

"Barry Screaming Mimi."

We laughed and hollered. Then we went quiet for a while. Lord, he's gorgeous, I thought as I watched him stretch out on the rag rug before the disused fireplace. I relit the joint that had gone cold.

"What are you thinking about, Sandy?"

"I don't know."

"Your face looked fantastic just then. Sort of sad. Can I take some shots of you?"

"Shots. What do you mean—take my picture?"

"Yeah."

"No way."

"Why?"

"I don't photograph well. I'm—I don't look good."

"Bullshit. Come on, sit for me."

"Forget it. Why don't you take Mia's picture? She's beautiful."

"I already did. I've got lots of Mia."

He began to pull at my sock then, tickling the underside of my foot, torturing me into agreeing to be photographed. I absolutely lost it, being the world's most ticklish person, and soon gave in.

I lay there, catching my breath, and Dan took my hand in his. For a split second I thought maybe he was going to kiss me, and I went rigid. I had never even dreamed of sleeping with any-body that good-looking. He didn't kiss me, though. Instead, he helped me to my feet. "Let's catch the light before it gets late," he said.

3

I DIDN'T DESPISE JACK KLAUS, THE WAY I DID THAT DETEC-tive Norris. But I didn't much like him, either. Klaus was another white cop, also a detective, and unlikely as it was, we had a few things in common—history of a sort.

Technically the history was between him and Uncle Woody. I didn't know what kind of favors one owed the other, or how the two came to know each other. I just knew Woody trusted him and they went back a ways. My uncle had called on Klaus to help untangle a couple of grisly South Side murders my family had been pulled into. Sure enough, Klaus had come through for us. He provided vital info from Chicago PD files and kept a great deal of heat off of me and Woody. When the smoke cleared he was being hailed as a supercop. He had earned a big rep for solving the crimes, and a big promotion to match.

His new digs on Taylor Street reflected it. Klaus, who was half Woody's age, had been appointed to a cushy spot in major crimes. He was sitting behind his blond wood desk when I came into the office. He cut his phone conversation short when he saw me, even stood to greet me. "It's nice to see you again, Cass."

I had been well brought up. Normally I appreciate that kind of courtesy. But I didn't return the greeting.

He had been nothing but respectful to Ivy, Woody, and me. And now he was being nice, going out of his way to look into Wilton's and Mia's murders. I just couldn't get up for being nice back to him.

I had to give him one thing: He sure looked more prosperous than he did the last time we'd met. Gone were the Robert Hall vines and the square haircut. He wore a nicely tailored suit—prison stripes, Nat called straight clothes—and his hair hung fashionably close to the collar of his crisp white shirt. Real sharp. Kind of like one of the actors on *The Name of the Game.* A long brown cigarillo rested on the lip of a brass ashtray near his hand.

I took out my pack of Multifilters, and he lit my cigarette.

"I understand they were friends of yours," he said. "You holding up okay?"

"I guess."

"Tough thing to be going through."

"Right."

He waited for me to expand on it. But I just sat there.

"You probably know I don't have jurisdiction in the case. I can only poke around, ask to be kept up-to-date."

"Okay."

"It's early in the investigation. But I was able to find out a few things anyway. I thought maybe you and me could catch some breakfast and I'd tell you about it."

"No."

"No?"

"I mean no, thanks. I don't want to keep you from your job. Can't we just talk here?"

He shrugged. "Sure."

He used the intercom to ask for coffee. A few minutes later, it was delivered along with a tray of sweet rolls.

"They don't have a lot to go on so far. There were plenty of prints and junk left in the apartment from the previous tenants. You and your roommates had all been in the empty place, too— and the maintenance guy who had the heart attack. All that just puts more BS in the game. And as you know, they haven't fixed time of death exactly. But before we get into what I know, let me ask you something, Cass."

"What?"

"What do *you* think happened? Any idea who could have killed them? Maybe they were dealing? They ripped off a supplier, burned the wrong guy. Something like that."

Burned, eh? Well, ain't you just the hippest narc in town.

"Is that what the police think?"

"It's in the running," he said.

I shook my head. "No way. Wilt and Mia didn't do that."

"Right."

He pressed a cherry danish on me, but I declined.

"It's pretty tense over your way since the riots. I mean, even now," he said. "We're looking at a lot of violence in that neighborhood. Shootings, holdups, muggings. You and your friends get along with—with everybody?"

"I don't know what you mean."

"Did your guy Wilton know any of the brothers from the projects maybe? Any of them ever come by the apartment to see him?"

"No."

"I'm wondering if any of the brothers ever give your friends grief?"

"Grief for what?"

"For living like you do—did. He had a girlfriend, after all, who wasn't the same race."

I didn't answer for a minute. His questions were rife with implications, all of them unimaginative and dumb. Probably the very dumbest was that young black males would actually be outraged that one of their own was screwing a white girl.

"Wilton knew lots of people," I said. "Far as I know, nobody resented him for being with Mia. Not because she was white, anyway."

"She was a pretty girl, they say. Some of the other guys in the house a little jealous of your friend Wilton?"

He was being cagey. Obviously he'd heard something about Barry and Wilt's rivalry. So it shocked me when he said, "Are you sure you never heard this Zuni threaten your friend Wilton?"

"Dan? What are you talking about?"

"Just wondering."

"Look," I said. "You people are wasting your time suspecting Dan. Not only did he think the world of Mia and Wilt, he wouldn't kill a flea if it was biting him."

He nodded, relit his brown smoke, which had gone cold.

"I mean it. Dan'll turn up in a day or two with a perfectly good explanation."

"Um-hum."

"Besides, has it occurred to Norris that somebody might have hurt Dan, too? He could have been grabbed or something when he left the house that morning. If you all have any smarts, you'll start looking at him as another possible victim."

"Good thinking. Any other thoughts?"

My chance to twit him a little. "There are these guys 'around our way,' as you say. These white guys who don't like freaks. Or black people. I heard they're the ones ripping off apartments. I heard a couple of girls have been raped."

He took that in. "Doesn't sound likely. Thugs like that, if they'd been watching the apartment, they'd have waited till you were all at home, and they'd have waited to catch everybody where you all live, not in a vacant apartment. No, this thing sounds much more personal. Lot of anger in this killing. Somebody really didn't like Wilton Mobley."

That sounded right. Unhappy as I was to have it said.

"Anyway," he said, "the chatter says it doesn't look like Mia Boone was raped."

"I'm glad," I said. For whatever it was worth.

"You looked so surprised when I mentioned Dan Zuni might've been jealous of your friend."

"Like I told you, that isn't true."

He opened a second container of coffee. "Cass, I told your uncle I'd do what I could for him. For you. And I meant what I said. Woody told me you'd cooperate in any way you can to help us nail whoever did this crime. Is that true?"

"What do you think?"

"So why don't you come clean about this fella Zuni?"

I tried to second-guess the man. Why in hell was he so convinced Dan had something to do with the murders? What kind of cop tactic was he pulling?

"Did you hear me, Cass?"

"I heard you. But you're not making sense."

"So it's news to you that Zuni and Mia Boone used to live together? You had no idea she was pregnant by him a couple of years ago? Had an abortion?"

I fell into a wordless stupor.

"Her parents even know about it. Mia Boone had a sister still living with her folks. Mia confided in her, made her swear not to tell anybody. But after the murder, the kid spilled the whole story to the parents. The way they told it to Norris, this Zuni was wrecked when Mia left him. Nobody can understand how he could have turned around and lived in the same house with her, watching her carry on with another guy. That'd be enough to make any man crazy jealous. Don't you think?"

I went on staring at his mouth even after he stopped talking.

"See what I mean, Cass? Either you want to help with the investigation or you don't. Holding out on us is not gonna cut it."

"I didn't know."

He pursed his lips.

"Look, I told you. I didn't know. But you know what? I'm not the one holding out here, trying to put something over on somebody. It's you. You're not helping me, you're helping yourself. You're acting like—"

"I'm just acting like a cop. That's all. So okay. We cleared the air on that. If you say you didn't know, then you didn't know."

Again he offered me the tray of sweet rolls, and again I said no. I was thinking about the one and only time I had been in Jack Klaus's home—the evening when he had smuggled out the official police files on an old, unsolved murder to show Woody and me. Klaus was pushing Sara Lee pound cake at me all night. Like some kind of demonic old-maid aunt.

Head down now, he thumbed through the papers inside the manila folder on his desktop. "At least you're in the clear," he said a minute later. "You spent the whole night with a Nathaniel Joffrey, I believe."

I said nothing.

"Jim Norris tells me you've got a lip on you but you're real smart, observant. I told him he was damn right."

"If Norris told me the sun was shining, I'd run out and buy a raincoat. Is that ox a friend of yours?"

"He does his job. And you'll probably be speaking to him again, so get used to it. You don't have to like him."

"That's a big load off my mind."

He bent over the papers again. "Alibis checked for Cliff Tobin and Beth Riegel. This fella Barry Mayhew can account for his whereabouts, too. But maybe he's bought himself a different kind of trouble. He was at some kind of LSD orgy. What's the story on him?"

"Didn't the police already get his story? They kept him at the station all that night, didn't they?"

"Yeah. But you live in the same apartment as the guy. I wanted your impression."

"I bet. Because I'm so smart and observant. You want me to snitch on Barry. Well, I'm not going to. Even if he is an asshole."

"Let's go over it again, Cass. If you're going to help with the investigation, you have to tell what you know."

"I'm not your snitch, man. I don't care how much you've done for Woody."

He sighed, exasperated. "Hey, Cass? I'm over thirty and I'm a cop; I'm the man, so you don't trust me for nothing. But take some advice, okay? Learn how to control that temper of yours."

"I'm going now." I stood up.

"Just a couple more—"

"I don't have to ask your permission to leave, right? I mean, you can't make me stay?"

"I can't make you do anything."

"Fine. I'm going now."

He sighed.

"By the way, Detective Klaus."

"You know better than that. Call me Jack."

"By the way, Detective Klaus. For future reference—it's not cool for just any old honky to call a black person 'brother.' "

I watched him turn scarlet before I ripped the plastic visitor's badge from my coat and stalked out.

4

EVERYWHERE I TURNED THERE WAS A BUILDING CONNECTED to the municipal bureaucracy. The courthouse. The county jail. Maybe even the chamber of commerce. I couldn't wait to get away from all that fascist architecture. The thing was, I didn't have the most highly developed sense of direction and after fifteen minutes I realized I was walking in circles. Trying to navigate my way to the subway, I somehow wound up in Chinatown.

Fucking Jack Klaus.

So, he thought I had a temper. He didn't know the half of it.

Should I even believe what he said about Dan and Mia? I wanted not to, but something in me knew it was true. Had Wilt known about them, too? Why hadn't he told me?

I stomped harder.

Every fear I'd had about the cops finding and surrounding poor Dan came back to me double strength now. It would be a horrible cowboys vs. the Indian scene. The death of Tonto, no kidding.

The sun was suddenly quite strong. That meant one thing: massive, flooding slush. My feet were soaking. When I spotted a bus with a number and destination that sounded the least bit familiar, I hopped on it. I figured I'd just take it to the South Side and maybe I'd be able to catch a jitney from wherever it let me out to Woody and Ivy's place in Hyde Park.

Within fifteen minutes I knew I'd done the right thing. I spotted Skip's Tavern, which wasn't far from my grandmother's Forest Street house. I got off the bus and started looking for a rogue cab. Across the street was Champ's, a legendary ribs and chicken joint. Looked like they were still doing great business. Customers were pouring in.

I even recognized one of them, knew him by the leather coat he wore. Barry Mayhew. The insensitive roommate who had never once mopped the bathroom floor or defrosted the refrigerator.

It took a couple of seconds to convince myself I wasn't dreaming. I even used the edge of my scarf to give a quick wipe to my eyeglasses. That was Barry all right. What the hell was he doing in what we reluctantly call the ghetto?

I couldn't imagine the answer to that. Any more than I knew why I found his presence in the neighborhood not just puzzling but ominous. But I was being foolish, I told myself. Champ's barbecue was probably the finest pork this side of Charleston. Barry was hardly the first white guy to trek across town for it. And besides that, I lived in the same apartment with him, for god's sakes. There was every reason in the world for me to go over and join him.

Not a chance. I backed into Skip's Tavern and went directly over to the window, keeping watch on the door at Champ's. I asked for a Miller and resumed the vigil.

Barry came out presently carrying a shopping bag with a grease spot on the side of it. Soul food to go. He walked briskly up the block. I saw him struggle a bit with the door to a rusted Volvo I recognized as Dan Zuni's heap.

I wasn't dreaming that, either. It was most definitely Dan's car. I'd been in it a dozen times.

Damn. Something was very wrong. There was a police dragnet out for Dan and his car. If they couldn't find the Volvo, how had Barry ended up with it? Maybe Barry had known all along where Dan was. Maybe he was hiding him someplace. And now he was . . . what? Bringing him an order of ribs for lunch?

For all I knew, Dan himself was in the car. Hunched down under a blanket on the backseat. Maybe wearing a false beard.

I threw a buck down on the bar, tore outside. But too late. Barry had already driven away.

The confrontation with Woody would have to wait. I ran to the el stop at 43rd and Indiana, eager to get home.

The ride was a long one, what with the change of trains in the Loop. I used the time to try to piece together some rational explanations for what I'd seen. I was stumped.

What should I do? Should I tell Taylor and Cliff and Annabeth I'd seen Barry in the Volvo? Or would that endanger Dan? I guess it was possible the others already knew, that I was the only one not in on the secret.

No, I was being paranoid. Wasn't I?

I hustled through the Jackson Street station, heading for the exit at Adams. I'd have to come above ground and then switch to the Ravenswood line. My thoughts were all over the place. I don't know how many times the young black man walking beside me had spoken before I realized he was talking to me. But now he was shouting in my face. "*Goddamn.* I said, 'Hello, sister.' "

I blinked at him.

"You sisters going up north are some stuck-up bitches," he called as he turned around and headed in the other direction.

I stood there like a clown, watching him until he disappeared around the bend. I guess I'd gotten so good at antagonizing my people that I no longer even had to do anything; my existence was enough to piss them off.

I was talking to Wilton once, probably bellyaching about some long-ago humiliation I'd suffered on the playground at Champlain Elementary School. I don't know, maybe the kids were goofing on my ugly brown shoes or the spastic way I was running after the volleyball. Anyway, when Wilt made fun of my misfortune, I gave him one of those *Et tu, Brute* looks.

"Cassandra," he said, "*niggers have it so hard. They need somebody to laugh at.*"

"*They have white people to laugh at, don't they?*"

"*I mean, besides whitey. See, the part that assimilated Negroes like you and me play? We actually give them somebody to feel superior to. And they're right, Sandy. They're better than us.*"

5

A BLACK-AND-WHITE WAS PARKED NEAR OUR BUILDING, A COP lolling behind the wheel. But I didn't pay him any mind. I was heading for the apartment lobby like a guided missile: My bladder was about to burst.

But then I saw Nat, his kindly face full of concern for me. I suppose my move was to run into the shelter of his arms. But I wasn't having any of it. I'd been dodging him ever since the murders. I put my hands up, palms out in a *halt!* gesture. "Get out of here, Nat," I said.

"Cassandra, are you crazy? Why won't you talk to me?"

"Go away."

"Go away? What am I, a dog you trying to get rid of?"

I didn't answer.

"Am I your fucking dog, Cassandra?" Not a trace of De Lawd's paternal solicitude, only venom.

"Look, I don't want to see you."

"Why is that?"

Because Wilton's dead and you're alive. But of course I couldn't say that. I spoke quickly to push the ugly, unreasoning thought out of my head. "I'm not going to get into it, Nat. Just leave me be. I need to go upstairs now."

"I'm coming with you."

"No!" The cop was interested in us now. He rolled down the window on the passenger side of the front seat. I smiled his way in an attempt to assure him there was no trouble, then lowered my voice. "You're not coming with me, Nat. Go home."

He stepped toward me, oblivious to the cop. "You stupid little girl. You got no goddamn idea." His voice was as far from the usual wheedling as it could get. Now it seemed to have a deadly black undertone.

"No idea about what?" I said.

He took another step forward, reached out. I took two steps back. He came at me again. I looked over at the cop, who was reaching for the door handle now. But before he could open the car door, and before Nat could lay hands on me, I turned and began to run. It didn't much matter where.

From the way Nat was calling my name, it sounded like I was doing the smart thing. It sounded like he wanted to strangle me.

I LEANED INTO THE DOORBELL. RANG IT SO HARD I MAY HAVE broken the damn thing. *Please, Owen,* I prayed. *Please be there.*

He had recently moved to the apartment on Menomonee, the

upper floor of a townhouse with lots of black iron grillwork and a little balcony. It was nicer than his old place, and several blocks closer to the commune. However, he was now located on the fringes of Old Town, which was expensive, tourist centered, and noisy; *plastic* was the all-purpose word for the area.

I rang harder, longer. *I know you didn't go home for Christmas break, Owen. You can't stand your father.*

Professor Owen Kittridge was one of the last reasons I had for staying in school. That was a real anomaly, because no other teacher missed so many days of classes. Half the time he was at home with a hangover. I suppose the chief reason the English department didn't fire him was his pedigree. Not many top Yale scholars wound up on the teaching roster of a small-potatoes institution like Debs College. The regents must've licked their chops when he accepted the post. Another reason he still had his job: In a time when so many of the younger profs were defecting to our side of the student-teacher divide, he was one of a handful of holdouts.

He was a good man of good conscience, but he was more or less apolitical, or maybe *suprapolitical* was a better word for him. You didn't find him at the Vietnam teach-ins, but he never failed to send in food and coffee to the forces occupying whatever official's office. He didn't picket, but he was always good for fifty bucks when the bail-raising committee knocked at his door.

He didn't knock points off your grade for poor attendance, either. Nor did he sleep with his students. What he did do, regularly, was smoke dope with them—with one of them anyway. Me.

Owen, a well-to-do white Southerner raised at arm's length by a patrician father and succored by a plump, live-in Negro nanny; classically educated and classically handsome; not as old as Nat but a good twelve years older than I; languid; traveled; easy in his body.

Me, a black Northerner; jumpy and seldom at rest; defensive;

odd-looking; born into poverty in the prototype urban slum; never been much of anywhere; bitter about what I didn't get; in the dark about so much of my past—all those family secrets— feeling haunted by it anyway.

But intense and unlikely friendships are a major theme in my life. Owen and I had been friends since I landed in his freshman comp class.

I heard footsteps—faint, Owen in those dumb Fred Astaire slippers of his—but yes, he was coming closer and closer to the front door. He was holding a newspaper when he opened up, his eyeglasses buried up in his hair.

There was no fooling me, though. He hadn't been reading the paper; he'd been asleep in his chair, nodding after a couple or four vodkas.

"I've been trying to catch up with you for days," he said. "Where have you been?"

"I've got to pee, Owen. Bad."

"Come on in."

There was never anything to eat at Owen's. Useless in a kitchen—that was one of the many things we had in common. Lipton tea was about the best he could do. I sat in the divine wreckage of his living room with the warm cup in my palms, filling him in on all that had happened, and apologizing for not being in contact sooner.

"None of it makes any fucking sense," I said at the end of the narrative. "I don't know what to do now."

"Pick up the telephone. Make your peace with Detective Klaus. Tell him what you saw this afternoon."

"I can't do that yet. Not until I know what the deal is with Barry and Dan. I rat on Barry and the police catch up with him and Dan. You know what Chicago cops are like. They could go in with guns blazing, no questions asked. Can you imagine how awful I'd feel? How guilty?"

"How awful would you feel if they had something to do with the murders and you let them escape?"

"That isn't possible."

"How do you know that? Leave it to the police. Please."

"That's the trouble, though. The police. Something isn't right. It's not right the way they're fixed on Dan as a suspect. And it's not right they haven't located him. Any more than it's right that Barry would be the one to stick his neck out by hiding Dan. I don't know, Owen. I don't feel good about telling them before I talk it over with Taylor and Beth and Cliff."

"Your loyalty to your roommates is admirable. But you're not a detective. Go home to your aunt and uncle where you can commence to mourn like anyone who's just lost a close friend."

"I'm loyal to Wilton. I'm not going to let go until I find out what happened. After that, there'll be lots of time for me to mourn."

"You've already started, my friend," he said. Then he got up to make himself a drink.

I didn't want one, so he brought me a club soda. I held it in my lap, not talking anymore. Owen sat next to me on the sofa and laid the inside of his hand gently across my forehead. "You need looking after."

"I'll be all right. You know, I'm loyal to you, too, Owen."

He smiled. "Don't think it goes unnoticed."

We were quiet for a while longer. "Is London nice?" I asked.

"Yes. I liked it a lot."

"God, I wish I were there now. I'd rather be anywhere, doing anything other than thinking about Wilt being dead."

"We could go to the movies. I'll see just about anything, except don't make me see *Bonnie and Clyde* again."

I let myself fall against him. "A friend is a miracle. Remember you said that?"

"Did I? I guess."

"I'm scared, Owen."

"I know. Why don't you lie down for a bit?"

I pressed myself closer to his heart. "You mean with you?"

He didn't answer.

"A few minutes of feeling safe," I said. "Being close, forgetting. Maybe you need that, too."

He didn't answer.

I straightened, moved away, too embarrassed to look at him. "I guess that's not what you meant."

"No. But—"

"It's okay. I shouldn't have said that. I'm a total feeb. If you were the least bit attracted to me, you'd have said so long ago."

"No, I wouldn't. I wish I could explain. This is hard to talk about."

"You bet it is. I'm sorry. I forgot there for a moment that I'm just goofy little Cassandra with the big legs."

"You're going to be a splendid woman. Maybe you can't see it just now. But wait a bit."

"You mean when I grow up."

"Sort of. You'll grow up, like you say, and be the toast of the town."

"What town would that be?"

"Somebody's town. Look, you're already breaking hearts."

"I never broke anybody's heart."

"Oh, really? Why don't you talk to Nat about that. Or did you forget what you just told me ten minutes ago?"

"Okay. I'm being shitty to him."

"And not particularly sorry for it, right?"

"I'll take a beer now, if you have it. But as long as we're on the subject . . . I mean, since I've already made a fool of myself, I may as well ask you something else. Once and for all."

"What?"

"Are you gay?"

"Excuse me?"

"I don't mean to insult you. But, are you, Owen? Annabeth thought I'd already slept with you, and when I told her we never did it, she said maybe it's because you're—well, gay."

"I'm not homosexual. Sometimes I'm not even sure I'm sexual. I kind of decided my uncle Jude was right about the wisdom of keeping to yourself."

"What does that mean? He never had sex?"

"Not as far as anyone knows."

"And that's what you want to be like? Are you nuts?"

He laughed.

"Was Uncle Jude a drunk, too?"

"Yes, of course."

"You know what I think? I think you're full of shit, Owen. I bet if Jane Hayer threw herself at you the way I did, you'd go to bed with her."

At the mention of his long-legged, curly-haired colleague, the Romantic Poets lecturer who always managed to seat herself near him at faculty teas, he looked away from me.

Dead giveaway.

"Oh, shit," I said. "How stupid could I be? You fucked her, didn't you?"

"Stop that."

"Oh, yeah, you did."

"Stop it. Listen, Cassandra, maybe you've been moving a bit too fast. Your transition from studious country mouse to foul-mouthed hippie chick might have happened just a little too fast."

And it isn't at all becoming, as my aunt Ivy would say. Too fast. I couldn't deny there was something in what Owen said. Where I had been shy and insular—what seemed like just yesterday—I was now brash and aggressive. And even I had to admit it didn't always feel right. It didn't always feel like me proudly rolling joints and setting up the communal bong like a pro, throwing around the four-letter words. The old Cassandra had to go. I knew that much. But sometimes I lost control of who I was replacing her with.

And now I'd made a clumsy pass at my beloved friend. He'd rejected me and I'd turned ugly. What unspeakable thing would I do next? Chase him around the room like an old lech in a Dagwood cartoon? He was right to put me in my place. Oh, God, I was mortified.

Owen tried to make me stay, but I wouldn't hear of it. I hurried down the stairs without a backward glance. I'd never felt more lumbering and unlovely in my whole life.

I had gone there seeking refuge, a way to stop thinking about the murders and everything else that was weighing on me, even if just for an hour. But apparently there was to be no rest.

No rest.

7

UNHINGED BY THE SCENE WITH OWEN, I STOPPED AT THE coffee shop on Lincoln Avenue and ordered a cheeseburger with onion rings and extra fries. No way to get slinky. But I forgave myself for the orgy of grease. I was ravenous. Before going to see Jack Klaus that morning, I had tried to eat a bowl of Mia's hand-mixed granola, but it stuck in my throat.

It had turned bitter cold again, and I'd lost my muffler somewhere. The powdery snow sifting down the back of my collar was like freezing ground glass. I pressed on along the darkened streets. The closer to home I got, the more watchful I became. I was afraid Nat might be waiting to ambush me again. Not only was I checking out the face of every man I passed on the sidewalk, I even began to look with suspicion at the cars moving slowly on the slippery road. Once or twice it seemed that a dark-colored sedan was keeping pace with me. I was being paranoid again. Stupid. Nat didn't own a car.

Chicagoans can't afford to be sissies about frigid weather. The shoppers going in and out of the neighborhood boutiques were bundled in hooded parkas and six-foot-long scarves, going on with their holiday errands despite the weather. I counted that as a blessing—plenty of people about.

Last year, about fifteen minutes after the release of *Sgt. Pepper*, head shops started springing up on every other corner of the North Side. In this neighborhood, if you run out of rolling papers or feel the urgent need at midnight for penny candy or a copy of the *Bhagavad Gita*, help is never far away.

The head shop is also a place to pick up the newest Kurt Vonnegut and sign up for a macrobiotic cooking class, buy a tarot deck or a framed photo of Chairman Mao. The geniuses behind the concept had a perfect read on the youth market. They'd hit on a brilliant way to merchandise to the anticonsumer sector.

The busy shop where Annabeth and Clea worked was called the Glass Bead, so named because the owner was an avid Hermann Hesse reader. But the Glass Bead had expanded way beyond the standard inventory of sandalwood incense and Top rolling papers. It now carried secondhand fur coats, Guatemalan ponchos, coffee beans from Africa, Dylan's last LP, or for that matter Dylan Thomas's last, India print bedspreads, straw tote bags from Mexico, hammered copper earrings, turquoise belt buckles. When good little hippies died they didn't go to heaven, they landed here on Lincoln Avenue.

A poster of the guys in Buffalo Springfield hung behind the counter where Annabeth, recently promoted to manager, stood sorting sheer cotton blouses into SMALL, MEDIUM, and LARGE piles. She was biting down on her bottom lip as she worked, her movements jerky and robotic.

That wasn't Buffalo Springfield on the sound system. It was Ravi Shankar. Annabeth seemed to lean into the music. It took a while for her to notice me.

"Sandy. I didn't see you."

"I know. You look—" I began.

"Yeah," she said. "Not so hot. You, too."

"I just wanted to get warm for a minute."

She laid her delicate fingers on my cheek, and then picked up my hand and began to chafe it. "Wow. You're frozen solid."

Annabeth was a classic slinky. Men had flocked to Mia's side, attracted by that willowy Mother Earth essence. But Annabeth, in her mini-minis and dangling earrings, was the kind of girl men flat-out lusted after. In fact, it didn't even seem right to call her a girl. Slinkies were women, not girls.

We stood there in silence for a minute.

Finally she asked, "You still freaking?"

"I barely know where I am."

"Yeah. Right on to that."

I stamped hard a few times, trying to shake out the numbness in my feet.

"Where's Clea?" I asked.

"She quit. She's so messed up behind what happened, she doesn't want to be anywhere near the commune now, or even on this side of town. I don't blame her."

I waited while she helped a customer.

"I didn't want to come to work today, either," she said. "I just wanted to stay inside the apartment."

I snorted. "Yeah. Safe inside our building. Where nothing bad ever happens."

She made a face. "You're just like him, Sandy. Even when something terrible happens, you can make a joke."

Just like him. She meant Wilton, of course. Time was, I'd be bursting with pride to be told that. Now it just hurt.

"But I guess you're right," Beth said. "It is spooky in the apartment now. What are we supposed to do?"

"1 don't know. It's shit either way."

She picked up one of the scratchy wool ponchos and wrapped it around her. "Speaking of shit . . ."

"What?" I said.

Detective Norris, red in the face, was walking toward us. "Cold enough for you girls?"

Neither of us answered.

"How's business?" he asked Annabeth.

"Pretty much like it was the last time you swung by here," she said. "I'm very busy. And, no, I haven't heard a word from Dan Zuni."

Norris turned to me then. "What about you?"

It was almost as if he was reading my thoughts. The second I saw him striding toward us, I flashed on Barry in the Volvo and my speculation that he might know exactly where Dan was. I hadn't even decided whether I should tell Annabeth about it, let alone the cops.

Another customer interrupted just then. Beth left me alone with Norris, damn it, whose eyes I couldn't meet.

"Did you hear me?" he demanded.

"Yeah, yeah, I did. Like she said, we don't know where he is. We're not hiding him in the basement or anything. Look. Wouldn't you be better off conducting a real investigation—trying to find out who killed Wilton and Mia—instead of hounding us like this?"

"Now, why didn't I think of that?" He took out his cigarettes, lit one, and let his gaze roam the store. "So this is where all the cute hippie chicks hang out."

"Hey, I'm serious, okay? You're treating Dan like he's public enemy number one, when he didn't have anything to do with those killings. But I'm telling you—don't hurt him when you find him. You'll be sorry if you do."

That got his back up. "Threat? You think your family's got that much pull with the PD in this city?"

"I'm not threatening you, Detective. I'm asking you to think."

"Yeah. Okay. You say he didn't do it, it must be so." I noticed that he was grinning now. "I'll tell ya. Your roommate's got a great little shape to her." The big creep was staring at Annabeth as she walked back toward us.

"I'm going home," I told Beth, and then turned to Norris, "unless you've got something else to say to us."

He took in a huge gulp of the dope- and incense-infused air. "Nope. Long as you understand you don't leave town until I say you can. You girls can finish your tea party now."

"Ha ha," Beth said when he'd walked off.

"I'm tired as hell, Beth," I said. "I'm gonna go."

"You okay walking home alone?"

"Yeah, I'm fine. Besides, there still seem to be uniformed cops everywhere. I guess they'd help out if somebody tried to snatch me."

"Are you sure? Taylor's picking me up tonight. I don't feel so great about closing up by myself. You could hang out until he gets here."

It just kind of burst out of me then. "Listen, Beth. I couldn't say anything while Norris was here, but . . . I mean, I don't even know if I should say anything, period."

"About what?"

"Nothing. Just come home with Taylor. We can talk about it then."

"You're scaring me."

"Be cool. I'll see you in a bit. I'm going to get out of here now. I'm beat."

She let me walk a few feet before calling to me. "I forgot. You know who else was here? Asking about you?"

"Nat."

"Right. Did you have a bad scene with him?"

I just shook my head.

"You're acting so weird. What's going on with you, Sandy?"

"Nothing. Everything. Like I said, it's all shit."

8

I MADE IT HOME WITHOUT ENCOUNTERING NAT. AND BY THAT time, the shame response was taking hold; I knew I should call him and apologize for the way I treated him.

Just the same, I took a cautionary look around before I opened the lobby door. And I kept looking back while I climbed the stairs.

But with all that, I let my guard down a few seconds too soon. When I reached our landing I took off one of my mittens and stuffed it into my coat pocket, which must have given the guy just enough time to fly at me like a hungry bird.

As soon as I had the apartment door open, he struck from behind. He shoved me inside and slammed the door shut after us. Before I could scream, a woolen gag was shoved into my mouth by a gloved hand. I tried to twist out of his grip but soon stopped, knowing my arm would break like old spaghetti. In a second my hands were tied behind my back. He executed it perfectly. When my legs gave way, he snatched me back up to full height. His garment was slick against me, and I could smell the snow on it. As he jerked my head about, my face brushed against the jagged metal teeth of the zipper on his jacket.

I had the craziest thought then: *If I have to die, at least I'll know who killed Wilton.* Because surely the same bastard who had murdered Mia and Wilt was about to slaughter me, too. Maybe I'd get a look at his face just before he did it. Be quick, you bastard. Just make it quick.

I was pushed onto the floor of the hall closet then. "Be quiet," he said. The way he whispered, those two words seemed to be the most horrible ones in the world. He locked me in.

I shivered and twisted as I sensed him roaming through the apartment.

After I'm dead, I told myself, Jack Klaus and the rest of them will be forced to get off their asses and find the murderer. Woody will make them find him. And it sure as hell won't be Dan Zuni with his bony frame and wrists like a girl's. No way. I was getting killed by a big strong man, thank you.

Then I heard the clang of metal in the kitchen, drawers opened and slammed closed again. Knives. The worst. Oh, Lord, he was going to cut my throat. I began to weep and pray and beg for my life, all that eloquence dying inside the spittle-soaked gag.

There came a ripping noise on the other side of the door. Close. He was so close now. The lock sprung. Doorknob turning ever so slightly. Sliver of light. The son of a bitch was good. He was downright theatrical. Maximum terror.

Pee began to soak my leggings. So undignified to leave this world pissing on yourself. But it couldn't be helped. I'd talked about so many things with Owen, with Wilton, with other people whose heads I respected. But not about how to die well. Get ready. People, get ready. The words to that Curtis Mayfield song made all the sense in the world now.

Then it all changed. And the change was beautiful. Now there was silence. Just silence. Oh my God, he was gone.

I waited another minute, nothing but my heartbeat for company, and then I began to buck and thrash for all I was worth. I fell out of the closet and used the knob to try to work out the knot in the rope around my wrist. I could see my knapsack on the floor of the living room. It was slit open, top to bottom, all my things scattered—notepad, Life Savers, lipstick, coin purse.

I sweated with the effort to free myself for a good ten minutes before I heard voices in the corridor. I stopped struggling, sat there waiting, mouth full of yarn.

The boy Jordan, usually so incurious, stared down at me in confusion. A second later Cliff appeared, face red, dripping snow, a Coca-Cola in one hand.

Apparently the two of them were going to stand there gaping at me all night. So I had to wake them the fuck up. I kicked out like a mule and barely missed shattering Cliff's ankle.

9

IT WAS ALL OVER NOW. CLIFF'S COMPLEXION WAS LIKE A RAW biscuit. He was scared out of his wits, but as the only man in the apartment, he took charge. The reluctant knight had a urine-soaked maiden and an underfed, semiautistic boy to look after.

First thing he did after untying me was to barricade the front door with a chair. Then he put Jordan and his bag of Jays potato chips into the living room. He came into my room, not even knocking first, caught me half-dressed, stuttered out his frightened question: "Sandy, were you raped?"

I shook my head.

"What did he do to you?"

I opened my mouth to answer, then closed it. "Nothing," I said at last.

"What?"

"He turned me into a sniveling, pathetic animal. But he didn't do anything to me," I shouted.

"Oh, man."

"Yeah."

"And you never saw him?"

"A fucking animal," I cried out. "No, I didn't see him."

It was queer. The softer his voice grew, the louder mine became. I screamed at poor Cliff, "What did he take?"

"Take?"

I peeled away from him, ran into the living room, the kitchen, Annabeth's room, the sunporch. Everything in place: the stereos, the half-dozen clock radios in the apartment, Taylor's watch, Barry's electric razor, household money in the flowerpot. He hadn't even stolen my wallet, which I found beneath the coffee table.

With Cliff at my heels, I opened the door to what had been Wilton and Mia's room. It was chaos inside. Drawers turned out, books swept from the shelves, throw rug turned over.

The scene terrified me all over again. But at least now it made some kind of sense. Now I understood. I saw that I had been in no real danger. Whoever that was, he needed to get inside the apartment and then neutralize me while he searched for something—literally, some *thing*. I had no clue what that could be. But it had something to do with Wilton and Mia. The guy even knew which room had been theirs. He had taken something we never knew we had. It had belonged to Wilton, or maybe to Mia, or, just possibly, to the thief himself.

I thought about the noiseless way the intruder had left, just crept away, how he'd unlocked the closet door and cracked it so that I could get air and get out. Almost like he was apologizing. It meant he'd found what he came for. Sorry for the inconvenience.

I was back in my body now. Fingers, toes, all there. Breathing free again. The relief came from knowing there had been some object to the guy's terrorizing me. I was also relieved, not to mention ashamed for even entertaining the idea, that it could not have been Nat Joffrey who'd done those things to me. Yes, for an instant there, at the very beginning of the assault, I had actually thought Nat, the professional pacifist, was mad enough to rape or even kill me.

Cliff got the kid into his pajamas and settled in his room.

"What's he doing here, anyway?" I asked. "I thought the county welfare people took him."

"They did. But Crash got him out last night. He told Jordan he was just going to the store this morning, but he's not back yet. Who knows when Bev's coming home. I didn't know what else to do."

"Is he flipping over what happened to me?"

"Ten years with those assholes, Jordan doesn't flip over anything. He just needs some sleep."

"There's something else, Cliff. Did Barry mention where he was heading when he left the house today?"

"I don't think so."

"And you haven't seen him since?"

"No."

"He's up to something. It's either a good thing—something brave—or something that stinks."

I started with the exchange I'd had with Jack Klaus and told Cliff everything that had happened during this singular day. I omitted my humiliation at Owen's place. But otherwise, I came clean.

"Did you call that cop Norris? Or the one you went to this morning?"

"No. And I'm not going to."

"Why not? Some crazy fuck tied you up. That's kidnapping or something."

"I'm not doing it, Cliff. I told you, the guy got what he came after and he won't be back. Besides, the police are doing a real bad number on us. I don't know what it is, but I don't trust them.

They're trying to frame Dan, and Klaus is some kind of front for them."

He didn't say anything for a while. He just looked sad, and kind of beaten.

"What do you think's gonna happen to Jordan?" he said finally.

"*To who?*" His irrelevant question enraged me. "How should I know?"

"I know. He's gonna have it awful. His life'll be shit. Probably end up hacking his foster mother to death."

"So now the biggest problem in our lives is Jordan?"

He pulled himself up slowly. "I'm sorry. I try to keep focused. But I can't. I'm too bummed out. I guess I'm just not as together as you are."

"Me? You think my shit's together? Cliff, that's a joke."

"No, it's not. You're the youngest one of all of us, but you're the one who's taking all the licks."

"I want to know why Wilton died. I have to know."

"Yeah, yeah. Believe me, I get that. But you're also keeping the rest of us together."

"I'm taking Mia's place, you mean."

"No. Not like her. In your own way. The thing is . . . It's over anyway."

"What is?"

"The commune."

"Why? Because I might move back in with my folks? So what? You guys lived here before I moved in. You can get other people."

He shook his head. "Nobody's gonna stay here, Sandy. Soon as the police close out the murder, we're going to break up. I know it."

"You can get another apartment."

"No. Taylor's got a woman now. He'll probably go live with

her. Beth's parents have money. She'll get an apartment in some fancy neighborhood, like they wanted her to do in the first place."

"And what about you?"

"I'll go home, I guess. I kind of want to anyway."

"You're not going back to school?"

"I could go someplace in Connecticut. I don't know. I don't care."

"Don't be stupid. You could get drafted. You want to go to Vietnam, man?"

He shrugged. "Cary went. They killed him over there, and the same thing'll happen to me. Who cares?"

"Come on, Cliff. Don't."

"Remember how we all used to be so fucking glad to be with each other? Bunch of people. All like each other. Respect each other. Wanna do what we have to do without all the hippie nonsense. Live right. Like Wilton used to say, Live right. That's how you change the world. Remember?"

"I remember."

"Well, maybe in the next fucking world."

All that anguish and cynicism just sounded pathetic coming from an overgrown boy in a green reindeer sweater. Cliff took a distressed-looking handkerchief from his back pocket and turned away from me while he blew his nose.

"Feel like smoking?" I asked.

"No."

"How about some hot tea?"

"I don't want it."

"Then make me some."

I ran a tub while he was in the kitchen, stripped out of my funky clothes and threw my leggings into the trash.

I peeked out of the bathroom door and saw him sitting quietly in the kitchen, staring at the steaming kettle.

Well, what now, Lord?

In a few minutes he came crashing in with the big yellow mug. "Ex-cuse me, going off like that. After what you went through, I shouldn't—God, I'm dumb."

"Cliff, you're in the bathroom with me. And I don't have on any clothes."

He set the cup on the toilet seat, and in the same gesture, it seemed, he had his arms around me. He pushed the hair away from my forehead, brought my face close to his. "Where're you coming from, Sandy? How'd you get to be so great?"

I didn't know what to say. But I noticed something I never had before. Cliff's eyelids. They were so light, it was as if you could blow gently on them and they'd float away, like that fuzzy flower that grew wild in the country.

He kissed me, kept on.

I began to cooperate. As he pulled me closer, I felt the damp wool of his sweater against my bare breasts.

"You never thought about me like this?" he said.

"No."

"No, I guess you didn't."

And his funny face was sweeter than I remembered, too, especially that lump at the end of his nose.

We kissed more.

"I did," he said. "A lot. I wanted to be with you a lot."

"I stink, Cliff. Wait."

"No. Don't make me."

Were we going to do it on the spot, standing up? Would we just roll into my room? Or were we going to try to fit our substantial young bodies into the tub?

I stepped into the warm water, and he pulled quickly out of his sweater and thermal undershirt. He picked up the sponge and began to soap me while I worked at the buttons of his jeans.

I had my hands on the last one, the pants just starting to slide off his ass, when we heard the ruckus. Annabeth and Taylor were pounding hysterically on the blocked door.

I splashed out of the tub, threw on a robe—I don't know whose it was—and hurried to let them in. With everything that had happened, I knew they must be thinking the worst.

10

TAYLOR WAS CARRYING AN OUTSIZE PIZZA. ONCE HE SAW THAT all was well, he began to ride Cliff for the makeshift barricade at the front door.

"Stop picking on him," Annabeth said. "Building a fortress sounds like a damn good idea to me. Let's get some plates, Sandy. I hate cold pizza."

But I didn't move toward the cabinet.

"What's wrong? Why do you look like that?"

"Somebody was in here," I said.

Taylor set the pizza carton down carefully, eyes on me.

"Somebody was in here. Tonight. He jumped me."

Annabeth stared hard at me. "What are you talking about? Cliff, what's she talking about?"

"I was jumped. After I left you at the store. He—tied me up." She moaned.

While I explained, she was taking it all in, but at the same time she was shaking her head, denying the words even as I spoke them.

Taylor stepped across the hall and opened the door on the devastation in Wilt and Mia's room. "Wow," he said slowly. "This is so fucked up."

Beth pulled herself together enough to ask, "What's taking the police so long? Where's Norris?"

I flicked my eyes over at Cliff, who walked away from me.

"I didn't tell the police. I'm not calling them."

And I thought Cliff's move on me in the bathroom had been sudden. Beth was on me faster than I could blink, not a bit interested in my theories about the intruder, why I was so certain he wouldn't return. She grabbed the collar of my robe and shook me like I was a free bubblegum machine. "Call them now. Call them now, or I'll do it myself."

"The hell you will, Beth. It didn't happen to you, did it? What are you going to say to them? How are you going to prove it?"

She broke away and snatched the kitchen telephone off the hook. I wrestled it from her hand.

"You're fucking crazy!" she shrieked. "You want to get us all killed."

I don't think she meant for her nails to dig into my cheek that way. But it took that sharp pain to kick me into action. I shoved her, and she stumbled on a chair leg. Then she righted herself and immediately came at me again. *"Asshole!"* she was shouting. "You arrogant cow." There was a lot of muscle behind all that slinkiness.

I'm no brawler. I may be kind of hefty, but I still fight like a girl. I went for her hair. Then we commenced to slapping each other. Oh, it was tawdry.

Taylor and Cliff handled us the way the refs on the Roller Derby treat those big women. I huffed and puffed from my corner of the room, all my goods hanging out of the torn bathrobe.

"The two of you," Annabeth said in disgust to the men, "can't you do anything with her?"

But they seemed to know better than to interfere. They only watched us, ready to break up the melee should it start again.

Finally, Annabeth was calm again. "Sandy," she said quietly, "you have crossed the line, hon. You're out there in space. You hear me? They took Wilton away from you, and it's made you insane. It's not your fault, okay? But you need help."

I knew I needed help. And I knew what I needed help with.

"Is that how your mom talks to her maid out there in Kenil-worth?" I said.

She threw up her hands then. "Fine. Be like that. But I'm not ready to die. If I don't get murdered in my sleep, I'm going home tomorrow."

"Oh, really? What's your friend Norris going to say about that? He told us—"

She gave me a toss of rich-girl hair. "I don't give a shit what Norris says. He's got a problem with that, let him take it up with my father."

We watched her as she slammed into her room and banged the door behind her.

Not even in my lurid imagination could I have dreamed up a scene like the one that had just taken place. Me and Beth Riegel fighting like cave women in a B movie. Another friend struck from the list.

And how was I going to make it right with Owen after what happened earlier? I couldn't imagine facing him again, but the loss of him as a friend would be the final blow.

As I slumped in the kitchen chair, swallowing back tears and clutching at the front of that stupid robe, all at once the exhaustion came down on me like a club. I knew I had it figured right: The intruder had what he wanted and wouldn't be back. Nobody was out to kill off this commune of hapless hippies. But I was so weary, if it turned out I was wrong, I didn't care just then. Kill me, I thought. Go ahead. Just let me rest.

Taylor and Cliff were talking, but their voices filtered down as if they were calling to me from the top of a hill. I dragged myself out of the chair and into my room.

11

WAS CLIFF RIGHT? WAS THE END AT HAND, OUR LITTLE EX-periment in democracy—living right—all over? Freedom, happiness, community all finished so fast.

I lay awake, staring up at the ceiling that Mia had painted a velvety blue and then overlaid with silver stars. When I joined the commune, that pretty make-believe sky had been her welcoming gift to me.

I imagined her up on the ladder doing that for me. Perhaps Wilt had helped, in his way, standing at the base of the ladder, holding it steady with one hand, smoking a joint with the other. It made my heart ache.

"Sometimes, when you're out with Mia, do black people ever look at you like you're a bug? Like you give them the creeps?" I asked him.

"Yeah," he said. "It's like you know what they're thinking. It's like, 'How can you stand them? How could you be with one of them, after what they did to us?' "

"And how can we?" I said.

Sleep overtook me at last.

GENTLY SHAKING ME AWAKE, CLIFF INTERRUPTED A VERY IN-volved dream I was having—not a good one. Bev, Jordan's mother, was in it. She was begging Barry, who was all dressed up like a medicine man in a bad western, to give her sick baby some kind of miracle potion.

I came to with Cliff's face looming over me. "What is it?"

"Beth called the cops," he said.

"Shit. They're here?"

"Not yet."

"Damn, she had no right!"

The pressure of his hand on my shoulder slowed my movements. "Just a minute, Sandy. I know you're mad and all. But I think Beth did the right thing. Some guy breaking in here like that—it's nothing to be playing around with."

"Who's playing? I'm not playing, Cliff. I told you he wasn't out to hurt me. He was looking for something in here."

"Even so, Barry didn't come home tonight. You've got to tell Norris you saw him in the Volvo. It's getting too fucking weird."

"I can't help that, Cliff. Why don't you tell Norris, or don't tell him. Whatever. Just let me get up, will you?"

"Wait, for Christ's sake. Don't you get it? *I* don't want you to go. I don't want anything else to happen to you."

His hand was now at the collar of my nightshirt. He leaned in to kiss me, but I stopped him. "What is this? More of what you said last night? You were serious about all that?"

"Yes."

"And you're fantasizing about what—you, me, and Jordan in a little cottage in the woods or something? You going to take us to Connecticut and we'll have a boat?"

He looked away, unable to deny it. And oddly enough, now that I'd said it, in theory there was nothing so terrible about the idea. I'd never been on a boat.

He got me while I was thinking. A long kiss like the ones we'd had last night.

"Why me?" I asked. "How come you didn't go after Beth . . . or Clea? Or somebody at school?"

"How many times do I have to say it? I want to be with you."

"All right. But it'll have to wait." I pushed out of bed then. "I'm splitting."

"Jesus Christ, Sandy. It's one o'clock in the morning. Where are you going?"

"Home, I guess. I mean, to Woody and Ivy's. I'll catch a cab."

"I'll come with you."

"You will not, Cliff. Now get out of here and let me get dressed."

CHAPTER FIVE

FRIDAY

WOODY WAS MAKING ME HIS FAMOUS APPLE PANCAKES. WHICH was mighty nice of him, in light of our last meeting. We had not talked since I freaked out on him and Ivy at the commune the day after the murders.

Ivy was still asleep. I had awakened the two of them at one-thirty in the morning, offering no explanation why I'd chosen that ungodly hour to come calling. I'll explain everything tomorrow, I told them, and we had all stumbled into our respective beds.

When I awoke in my old room about 9 A.M., I could smell the sausages and coffee. I followed my nose out to the kitchen and found my uncle, fully dressed, sleeves rolled up, sifting flour into an old crockery bowl.

I hardly knew where to begin, how to apologize. After a

minute of fumbling for the words, I gave up, lip trembling, willing myself not to bawl like a baby.

Woody put down his wooden spoon and came over to me, hugged me tightly. "You will always be my girl," he said, and there may even have been a bit of wetness in his eyes.

"But," I said when I'd brushed away the tears, "you still think I'm foolish to get all up in this murder thing, don't you?"

"I wish you wouldn't, Cass. But I can see you're going to do it anyway. So I have to stand with you."

The pancakes didn't disappoint. They were just as delicious as I remembered. Truth was, Woody was a better cook than Ivy, who had help with the household stuff several days a week. But on lazy Sundays or holidays, Uncle Woody would prepare one of his specialties—pancakes, or pepper steak, or his sensational duckling in sweet sauce.

After eating, we sat at the kitchen table over our coffee. Woody lit a cigarette with his beloved old Zippo. "Jack tells me you came to see him."

"Yeah, I did." I hoped Klaus hadn't gone whining to Woody, telling him how rude I'd been, or that I'd stormed out of his office.

"He says some things are coming to light about these two youngsters. Details about the deaths. It's not nice, Cass."

"I didn't think it would be."

"He says the boy was tortured before they killed him." Tortured. Jack Klaus was right: That was *personal*, I thought. "But it looks like they killed the girl right off. The homicide detective thinks she might've just walked in on it."

I swallowed hard, refusing to visualize any of it.

"Cass, doesn't common sense tell you somebody was trying to get something out of that boy he didn't want to give up?" he said.

I nodded.

"Must have been a pretty big secret he was keeping."

"Wilt didn't keep secrets."

"You sure about that?"

I hesitated before answering. I was thinking about what Klaus had revealed yesterday—the old relationship between Mia Boone and Dan Zuni. That was a secret, wasn't it? But I didn't know whether Wilt was party to it.

Almost as if he was reading my mind, Woody said, "Cass, you were devoted to this boy. But you have to ask yourself some hard questions. You say you knew him so well. But is that really true? What kind of things was he doing when you weren't with him? Who all was he associated with? What about his friends?"

"His friends were my friends. We all lived together."

"I don't mean them. The boy lived in Chicago all his life until he went to school, didn't he?"

"Yes."

"Did he get into any kind of trouble while he was away?"

"He never told me about anything like that. Neither did Taylor. They were at school together. I'm sure the police asked him about that."

"Maybe he had enemies here in the city, people you don't know about."

"It's hard to think of Wilton having enemies."

"Don't be childish. Everybody's got enemies. Young men get up to things they don't want other people to know about. Especially colored boys in these times."

"Oh, look, Woody. Wilt was no criminal. His mother and father have money, and they sheltered him all his life. He went to the Lab School and Francis Parker. His dad is Oscar Mobley, one of the biggest, richest lawyers in the city."

"You don't have to tell me who Oscar Mobley is, girl. I'm the one can tell you about him. And one thing I'll tell you is, it's a good thing he is a smart lawyer, because he was able to get your boy out of trouble with the law."

"What trouble?"

"Drug trouble. Wilton Mobley was arrested for selling dope to his classmates."

"Oh."

"You didn't know that, did you?"

"No. But so what? Selling a little grass. That's no big-time crime. I know lots of people who do it."

"Is that so?"

"I mean, he couldn't have been a major—Wilton didn't have a lot of money. His mother slipped him cash sometimes. And he worked sometimes at the bike shop. People who sell in a big way make thousands."

"You know all about it, I see."

"All right, Woody, don't blow your top over this. I only meant that . . . that lots of people are into smoking marijuana. Re-spectable people. Wilton probably gave away as much as he sold. I mean, it's not the same as heroin. I mean, there are some places where it isn't even illegal."

No way to back out now. Oh, what a pile of shit I had stepped into. I might just as well have come out and said I smoke dope on a regular basis.

"You see what I'm talking about, Cass? You didn't know this fella near as well as you thought you did. Just like you didn't know the white girl he lived with had been with that boy who's missing."

"I see Jack Klaus has been bending your ear."

"Yes. Isn't that what you want? Somebody on the inside who can tell us the straight story?"

"Straight? You think he's giving me the straight anything? I don't trust him, Woody."

"That's too bad. Because you need him."

"I don't know if that's the kind of help I need."

"Well, I do. If you think you'll get anywhere without him, you're crazy. It's only because of Jack that the homicide man didn't pull you in for being uncooperative. This Norris fella thinks maybe you haven't told him everything you could."

To put it mildly.

I sat tight. Norris was going to have calico kittens when he got to the apartment and heard the third-hand account of the break-in and assault on me. Most likely he was looking for me now. Cliff was the only one I'd told where I was going. I knew he wouldn't fink on me.

Uncle Woody wasn't going to be thrilled that I was holding back that information from him, too. I'd tell him about the break-in, but in my own good time. If I spilled it now, he'd stop at nothing to get me out of the commune and back to Hyde Park.

"All right, Woody. Klaus or no Klaus, everybody seems to be looking for a way to blame Wilton for what happened to him and Mia. Which is insane. I don't care if he was Al Capone. That doesn't make it okay for somebody to murder him. Or do you think that's a childish notion, too?"

"No" was what he said. *Why can't you be eleven years old again?* was what I saw in his face.

"Let's back up here for a minute, Cass. There's something we didn't finish talking about."

"Dope, you mean. Look, Woody—"

"No. Not that. I asked you about his friends outside of your roommates."

"Honest, I didn't know about his old friends. Except somebody named Alvin."

"All right. Who was this fella Alvin?"

"I couldn't say. Wilt used to talk about him when he was kind of putting himself down. Almost like he idolized him. 'Alvin was tough.' 'Alvin was a real black man.' 'Alvin knew what was really going on in this country.' Things like that."

"But you never met the boy?"

"No."

"So this Alvin is a tough young nigger who knows everything, huh? Sounds like he could have been showing your friend the ropes in the dope trade."

"Stop making things up. The guy isn't a pusher. He was in Vietnam."

"So maybe he's not caught up in drugs. But he still could be one of *them*."

Them. I knew what that meant. "God, Woody. Don't go off on one of your raps about the black nationalists. Please."

He looked at me grimly. But he didn't say any more. Maybe he was following Ivy's old advice to me: When you feel like you're losing your temper, take some deep breaths and don't say a word until you calm down. "No last name on Alvin?" he said evenly.

"I don't think Wilt mentioned it. He might have, but I've forgotten it."

"Okay, young woman." He started to clear the table. "You realize, don't you," he said, "you've got a duty to perform. It won't be pleasant, but it's the decent thing to do. If you felt like you say you did about Wilton Mobley."

"What are you talking about?"

"You should pay a call on his people. When were you planning to do that?"

He was right. He was absolutely right. "I'll do it now."

"The boy was angry at his father, you said."

"The other way around. They were angry at him. They were trying to make him go back to Antioch."

I came in for a bit of his caustic commentary then. "Imagine that. Man spending his hard-earned money to give the boy an education, try to get him started in life. And that fool has the nerve to wipe his feet on it. Yeah, that's the big problem these days. None of you young folks like to be told what to do. It's always gotta be your way. You know better. We don't know a god-damn thing."

He smoked without talking for a few minutes, then said, "Anyway, you get on over there to see those people. Sim will take you."

"Who?"

WOODY ALMOST ALWAYS USED A—WELL, IT'S MORE THAN A little pretentious to call him a chauffeur—a driver, is what I mean. The previous one, whom we called Hero, had been with him for years. He was Woody's nephew. Hero had had more than his share of problems, among them his lengthy and wasting drug addiction; but in the end he surely lived up to his nickname. He had met that end on the street one night, killed by one of two men who attacked Woody and me. Hero died saving us.

"Cass, this is Sim," Woody said. "He's helping me out these days."

The same kind of help Hero had provided, I presumed: accompanying Woody while he went about his business, known and unknown, all over the city. Or just waiting for him in the Lincoln while Woody lunched with his cronies. And if any kind of muscle was required for the job, it looked as if this guy Sim could handle it. Unlike undernourished Uncle Hero, he was big.

"Hi, Sim," I said as I got into the backseat.

He was wearing a light-brown suede jacket and a yellow shirt. His dark hands resting on the steering wheel were huge and shapely like a basketball player's. He turned around, eyed me for a few seconds, like he was memorizing my face or something. "How you doing?"

Woody moved to close the door after me.

"Aren't you coming?" I asked.

He shook his head. "Last thing in the world I want to see is a mother who just lost her boy. Very little in the world is worse than that."

He should know. Aunt Ivy had miscarried twice and delivered one stillborn before they gave up trying to have children.

"When you talk to his folks," Woody said, "you gotta know what you're doing, gal."

"What do you mean?"

"I mean, you're in a position to talk to the Mobley family like the police won't. They can't. For one thing, they wouldn't know how. For another, they don't care like you do. But you have to be careful of these people's feelings. Realize what they going through. If there's any chance they can shed light on the killing, you gotta get them talking. The boy was theirs. They should be able to tell you who he was. And if you come to find out they didn't really know him much better than you did, well, so be it. That's gotta mean something, too. You understand?"

"I think I do. You're telling me pretty much what Jack Klaus told me. Either I want the truth to come out or I don't. I have to find a way to stand back from Wilt. Be hard on him and be hard on myself."

"Now you're talking."

Was I? I hoped it wasn't just talk.

2

HYDE PARK IS ONE OF A VERY FEW COMMUNITIES IN THE CITY that people like to describe as "integrated."

True and not true. Of course, the mighty University of Chicago is the chief explanation for the variety of colors and ethnicities on the streets. Students and faculty come there from all over the world. Mixed couples strolling with their café au lait babies don't raise many eyebrows. And solid, well-to-do Negroes long ago established a beachhead in the area. Still, blacks not connected to university life, and even some who are, usually get shut out of the more desirable housing. The real estate guy who was so nice when he showed you the sunny two-bedroom place? You'd be ill advised to sit by the phone waiting for him to call you back.

Wilton's parents were not only longtime Hyde Park residents, they had crossed the neighborhood's Maginot Line, the little enclave of Madison Park. They lived on a street so hincty that many of the realty ads for homes along its lovely, tree-shaded blocks state boldly: PHYSICIANS AND PROFESSORS ONLY. OTHERS NEED NOT APPLY. My great-aunt and -uncle were quite comfortable, but they had never lived like the Mobleys, and although Ivy had been introduced to Hope Mobley once or twice, she was not part of her rarefied social set.

Sim found a parking spot near the corner of the street. I got out of the Lincoln and walked to the moss-covered house where Wilton had grown up. I took a minute to prepare myself before I rang the doorbell. I'd be entering a house of mourning where emotions would be running high. I had managed to keep myself together this far, but there was a danger of falling apart once I was face-to-face with the grieving parents.

A small, plain woman in brown gabardine answered the door. Wilt must take after his dad, I thought at first. Then it registered: This is the maid. I gave her my name and asked if the Mobleys might have a few moments to see me.

Hope appeared a second later, before the first woman even had time to announce me. As expected, she was long and slim and handsomely coiffed. In fact, all my predictions about her seemed to be on the money. Just as I'd thought, she was dressed in costly black wool, and she looked devastated, emptied out.

But I hadn't expected her to trip on the Persian carpet in the entryway. She went sprawling, and then just sat there. Her expression never changed.

Wilton said a fair amount of drinking had been going on in the house ever since he could remember. I figured his mother must be dulling her pain with alcohol. I ran to her, reached down to help the maid help the mistress. But there was no telltale liquor breath.

I heard the word *no* spoken simply and with absolute finality.

Oscar Mobley, who had thundered that word, was suddenly at the bottom of the staircase. He was considerably shorter than his wife, but in his severe dark suit he cast a long shadow. His voice carried the same kind of spooky authority that I sometimes heard in Uncle Woody's. But if you met Woody's eyes when he was riled, the fire there could scorch you. Not so with Mr. Mobley. His eyes were cold glass. The name of a film Owen once took me to popped into my head. *Day of Wrath.* Mr. Mobley had *Day of Wrath* eyes.

I backed away while he drew his wife to her feet and then led her off.

The woman in brown showed me into a wonderful room with a fireplace and burnt-orange leather seating. Across the room was a massive console with a Grundig hi-fi setup. Hundreds of LPs filled the built-in shelving at knee level. Leontyne Price, Beethoven, and Duke Ellington seemed to be more than fairly represented. No music in the room now, of course. But no other sounds either, not anywhere in the house. No sound, no lights burning, but a faint and dimly familiar odor. White tulips in a giant urn, but they had no scent. Oh, yes, now I had it. That faint smell was furniture polish—butcher's wax.

Mr. Mobley had to be just as devastated and inconsolable as his wife. He had his own way of showing it. No clumsiness in him. Deliberate movements. A curt nod and a slight bow to me.

Funny—the first time, he made his entrance with the word *no*. This time, he said "Yes?"

He had wasted no words. But when I told him who I was, his vocabulary expanded quickly enough. I said his eyes were cold. Make that glacial . . . arctic . . . polar.

"I see," Oscar Mobley said. "You're one of the doping morons he chose to throw his life away on."

The loathing in his voice brought to mind an incident I hadn't thought about in years. The first time I was allowed to ride the el all on my own, I promptly got lost, found myself way the hell out around Western Avenue. Two white girls were giving me filthy looks, laughing at me behind their hands. One of them kept glancing at me and then holding her nose as if she smelled something foul.

I guess I had about the same reaction to those bitches that I had now. Hurt, trembling humiliation turning bit by bit into impotent rage. Wanting to strike out but also wanting to crawl into a hole.

I cleared my throat. "Wilton didn't throw his life anywhere, Mr. Mobley. His life was taken from him."

"You have the audacity to be impertinent with me? At a time like this."

I needed to measure my words, remain respectful. I knew that. Even if he was making no sense and looked as if he wanted to rip my throat out.

"I think you're misinterpreting. I only meant that the police think whoever did this had some reason for targeting Wilton. It wasn't a matter of how he lived, or where or with whom. I think so, too. Oh, never mind that now. I only wanted to tell you how sorry I am. And I thought I might be some help to you at the service."

"*Service?* You're not coming to any service."

"I can't come? But why?"

"You will be no part of it. Stay up north with those other hooligans."

My God. So my last image of Wilt would be that bloody torso lashed to a chair. Boy, that hurt me so much, I nearly bent double.

"Okay," I said. "Forget about the funeral. But don't you at least want to hear how much we all thought of Wilt?"

"I don't want to hear a goddamn thing. What are you going to tell me about? How much marijuana you smoked at those degenerate parties he was throwing? Your criminal enterprises? I know everything I need to know about all of you. You think justice will come at the point of a gun. You'd rather act the fool than put your shoulder to the wheel. You want to tear down everything we built with our blood and tears."

Blood and tears. Where was all the purple rhetoric coming from? His manner was flipping from heel-clicking hussar to country preacher. The guy must've been waiting a long time for somebody to dump all this on.

My temper was rising like a doughnut in hot oil. "Mr. Mobley, I don't know what you're talking about."

"Oh, the hell you don't. You lazy, raggedy—living up north with the worst kind of decadent white do-nothings. You people have got no decency in you, no more morals than a farm animal. God knows what kind of place you're from."

Okay. I'd had it.

"I'm from a place where I was taught to have some basic kindness and manners."

"That much is clear," Hope Mobley spoke as she stepped into the room. "I'm sorry to keep you waiting. Please have a seat."

Mobley turned on her, furious at her invitation, but she just shook her head at him. "What you're doing won't help, Oscar. Go someplace. Go upstairs."

He bellowed at her, "He wasn't welcome in this house. Now, why in hell should I have to entertain one of them?"

She shook her head again. "Go on up," she said mildly. "Go upstairs and hide your face. You'll be all right."

She waited with her eyes lowered until he left the room.

Wilt sometimes referred to his father as a pompous shit. I had no trouble seeing why. But that didn't keep me from pitying the rigid, heartbroken man.

"Will you—I'm sorry, what was your name?" Hope asked.

"Cassandra."

"Will you excuse me, Cassandra, if I don't offer you refreshments?"

"Of course I will."

"Yes, you seem like a nicely raised child. I thought you could understand."

"Yes, ma'am, I can."

The old fantasy had me charming the pants off the Mobleys, making peace between them and Wilt. I'd make out a case for our choices: Yes, we wanted out from under their supervision and their set of morals; yes, we were impatient with the high-cost education they were underwriting; yes, we liked the idea of a handpicked family rather than a biologically determined one. But none of that meant we dishonored their generation and all its sacrifices—blood and tears, if you must. Oh, I was going to be wildly articulate, and I was going to be Exhibit A, Wilt's lovely little friend, a nicely raised child.

"I know I'm intruding, Mrs. Mobley. All I wanted to do was bring my condolences."

No wonder I mumbled those lines. I was lying. In part, anyway. I did want to show sympathy, but I was also looking for information. I hoped she had enough left to give it to me.

She repeated my word. "Condolences." It had the ring of a melancholy musical piece, something by Scott Joplin.

"Can you stand to hear me out?" I asked. "And then I'll go."

"What is it?"

"Your husband talked about wild parties and criminals. Like Wilt was doing something wrong and should have expected to get hurt. What does your husband know that I don't?"

"What does it matter anymore?"

"It matters. I can see you being so hurt that you can't think about that now. But it matters to me."

She looked at me closely, maybe seeing me for the first time. "Did you know the girl he was living with?"

"Mia. Yes."

She faltered, and I rushed in. "She was a good person. He was happy with her. Believe me."

"Well, that's something, at least. All right. I'll tell you what Oscar was ranting about, if it will do any good. My father had a home in Kent, Michigan," she said. "It's on the lake. We used to spend summers there. When he died, he left the property to me. We don't get up there very often, not for the last few years. We pay a man in the town to look in on the place from time to time. My husband received a call from him a while ago. He had noticed cars parked on the property from time to time. It looked as though someone was using the place regularly, and he wanted to know if he should continue to go in and check the pipes.

"Of course, we had no idea what he was talking about. We thought at first the house was being burglarized. But Oscar questioned Wilton and got him to admit he was the one who'd been using the place. He'd been bringing friends up for—well, I could imagine what for. I take it you weren't one of the guests."

"Definitely not," I said. Nor was anybody I knew.

"Oscar was furious. Wilton promised him he wouldn't do it again. But when Oscar made a trip out there to check up on him, he found evidence Wilton lied to us. It was obvious the place was still being used. Oscar went off the deep end. He told Wilton if he ever went there again without our permission he'd have him arrested."

"That's a little harsh, isn't it?"

"I said he found 'evidence,' because that is the word Oscar used. But he didn't just mean dirty dishes and the leavings of a few marijuana cigarettes."

"What else did he find?"

"I don't know. He wouldn't discuss it with me. But he and Wilton fought like wild animals about it. I thought it would blow over like the other trouble between them in the past."

"What trouble was that? Selling grass to his high school buddy?"

"Yes. Oscar had to extricate him. But this thing with my father's place was altogether different. I just know that my husband had been talking wild the last two weeks, saying things I didn't understand."

"Like what?"

"That he'd pulled our son back from the edge for the last time. That Wilton's behavior was jeopardizing his law practice and his reputation. He even said if Wilton didn't change his ways, he'd—"

I supplied the words. "He'd kill him."

"That's right. Kill him. He said it the way every parent on earth has ever said those words. Except now . . . well, now he's left with all that on his heart. You saw for yourself what it's done to him. And me."

"You have no idea what they were arguing about? What Mr. Mobley found in the house?"

"No. He won't tell me."

I knew how much chance there was of his telling me.

"Anything else you can think of? Old fights with people? Anyone ever threaten him? Any chance his death was connected to your husband's affairs, or even yours?"

"No, none of those things."

"Is your husband pushing the police to find out who killed Wilt?"

"Yes, Oscar is trying to throw his weight around. Another way to assuage his conscience. I doubt that he's frightening anyone, though. He's defeated. It took this to defeat him."

"Your husband's not used to being defeated, I imagine."

Her mouth pulled suddenly to one side. "No," she said, "he isn't."

Oh, man. All the things Wilt had told me about the unhappiness in this house—they couldn't have been even half the story.

Hope saw me to the door a moment later.

"One more thing," I said. "Well, actually two. Did Wilton have a friend named Alvin? Or has your husband mentioned that name?"

"No. Who is he?"

"I'm not sure. The last thing is, it looks like we'll all be moving out soon. I'll have Wilt's things sent to you if you want."

"That's very nice of you. I'd like to give you something, too, to remember him by. I have some very sweet old photos. But I don't think Oscar would like that."

"It's not important."

It didn't feel right to have that phrase hanging in the air between us. I didn't want that to be the last thing I said to her. I wanted to tell her I needed no snapshots of him, my life would be over before I forgot Wilton. But while I was trying to figure out some beautiful way to say it, the door closed behind me.

Looking closely at the dense, ice-laden moss on the facade of the house, I could see there were tiny Christmas tree lights intertwined with the greenery. But of course, they were dimmed now.

I walked back to the car. When I didn't get in immediately, Sim looked out at me, waiting, but said nothing.

I was thinking about the quiet little town of Kent. One of those posh villages, like Martha's Vineyard, where moneyed blacks had established an enclave in the early part of the century, the houses passed down from one generation to the next.

Evidence. Whatever it was that Oscar Mobley found at the house, it had sent him into a real tailspin. And as for the so-called friends Wilton had been partying with up there—who were they? He'd surely never invited anyone from the commune, not even Mia. I wasn't just feeling left out, though; I was feeling betrayed. Here was another secret he hadn't let me in on.

Tough. I had to get past that. I said I was willing to face the truth no matter what came out. If I hadn't meant it before, I did now.

Jack Klaus had intimated that Wilton may have burned a drug connection. I didn't buy it. But I knew who might have done something like that: Barry Mayhew.

Oscar Mobley found out there were some funky dishes and funky doings at the house in Kent. But maybe the people up there weren't partying. Maybe they were cooking up something else. *Better living through chemistry.* That was a slogan my little generation had taken to heart. Find an isolated spot and put a couple of talented chemistry students to work. There was a fortune to be had. That sounded like a possibility, too. Once again, I smelled Barry. Maybe he had been the one member of the commune to be asked up to Kent.

I opened the car door. Not the rear door, the passenger side in front. Sim asked no questions except, "Where to?"

3

THE WINTER SUN CAROMED OFF THE DELUXE APARTMENT buildings along Lake Shore Drive. Not to get too sappy about it,

Lake Michigan can be pretty damn thrilling sometimes. But the majestic expanse of it is no watery womb. Stretching on forever, frozen blue, it looks ungiving, fatal.

"The lake's amazing, isn't it?" I said. "Do you ever just sit and stare at it?"

"Naw."

I was looking at the water. Sim was looking at the road.

"You know Skip's Tavern, on Indiana?" I asked as we cruised past the 25th Street exit.

"Uh-huh."

"How about having a drink with me at Skip's?"

"I don't know about that."

"Because of Woody, you mean. He lets you take a break sometimes, doesn't he?"

"Yeah, I take a break. But not to drink."

"Lunch then. We could go to Champ's and you could get something to eat there. My treat. You like their ribs?"

"They okay."

He found a place to park on Forest Street. Just my luck.

When he stepped out of the car, he seemed to emerge in sections. His chest was massive, his thighs like pillars, canoe-size feet in dark-brown boots.

"See that next block?" I said to him. "I was born on that block. Or somewhere near. Anyway, that's where I used to live, with my grandmother."

He nodded.

At the red Formica table we hooked, Sim papered his starched yellow shirtfront with napkins and tucked into the ribs. I marveled at what a fastidious eater he was, not a drop, not a splash of barbecue sauce on him. I ordered a dish of banana pudding, only two or three million calories' worth.

He never asked why I was so eager to buy him a meal. I guess he knew that I was after something. While he ate, I got up and went over to talk to the waitress and the fry cook. Sim didn't ask why I was doing that, either.

"How long have you been with my uncle?" I said when I came back to the table.

"Since July."

"You like working for him?"

He grunted.

"Sim. What is that short for? Simmons?"

"My mama named me Simpson."

"Sim, you mind if I ask you a few personal questions?"

I got a few blinks out of him, but no answer. Still, I pressed on. "You do any drugs?"

"I look like a junkie to you?"

"I don't mean that. I'm talking about grass, hash, coke."

"Why you wanna know that?"

"I have my reasons. And don't worry, I would never say anything to Woody."

"I like to get high. Who don't?"

"When you buy it, do you get it from somebody around here?"

"You wanna cop? You didn't have to buy me no ribs for that."

"I don't need to—" I stopped myself. "Actually, yes. That's what I want to do. Cop. Can you put me in touch?"

He had methodically eaten all the ribs before going after the french fries. Now he was taking care of those as he thought it over. "What if your uncle find out? Good-bye to my job."

"He won't. It'll all be on me."

"Okay."

"Can I ask you something else? You've been in prison, haven't you?"

He was using a Wet-Nap to clean his face. The little square of moistened tissue was lost in his big hand. "You say you was raised around here?"

"Yes."

"Y'all are some nosey motherfuckers in this neighborhood."

WE PICKED OUR WAY AROUND THE MOUNDS OF FILTHY SNOW.
"Your connection," I said. "Is he just some kid who deals on the
street?"

"I don't buy from no kids."

"All right, don't get mad. So your connection is a little higher
up on the chain. Does he work for a man named Henry Waddell?"

Now Sim looked at me with something other than that impas-
sive stare.

I repeated it. "Does he?"

"Not much get sold on the South Side Waddell don't have
something to do with."

"So that means yes. Your guy works for Waddell. Even if it's
indirectly."

"Even if it's what?"

"I'm saying your guy may not take orders directly from Henry
Waddell. But Waddell will end up getting his cut."

"Damn right he will. How you know about that anyway?"

"I'm not as dumb as I look, Sim."

"Didn't nobody say you was dumb."

"Lame, then. I'm not as lame as I look. You think I'm some
boogie college girl living up north and I don't know shit about
the haps around here. But I've actually met the famous Mr. Waddell."

"Yeah, I believe that."

"It's true, I have."

I wasn't going to go into the story now, but I had made the acquaintance of the South Side drug lord earlier in the year. When my Aunt Ivy lay near death in the hospital, Waddell had shown up out of the blue. In a heartbeat, he and Woody were at each other's throats. They clearly hated each other, and it was soon apparent that the enmity went back to a time long before I was born. I pestered the hell out of Woody until he leaked a few details about Waddell—his low morals and his high standing in the crime community. But he wouldn't give up any of what I sensed was the juicy saga of their personal relationship. I just knew that Ivy figured into it somewhere. Love triangle? Secrets carried up to Chicago from someplace down south? I had no idea.

"I'll tell you about Waddell some other time," I said. "But for now, what's your guy's name?"

"Jones."

"Now, that's an unusual name. Really distinctive."

Sim halted and put out his arm to stop me walking as well.

"Don't you be talking like that to this dude," he said.

"Like what?" I said.

"Like screamin' on his name and shit. He ain't gonna think that's funny."

I was suitably chastened. "Okay."

Jones ran his operation out of the back of a barbershop. All four chairs were occupied. Three afros and a shaved head under way.

I waited up front, leafed through an ancient *Life* magazine, and let the four barbers check me out while Sim went on back to score. I didn't just want him to buy grass for me; in fact, I didn't want the grass at all. What I needed was Henry Waddell's address.

As I waited for Sim, I couldn't help pondering my sexual fate—again. When I wanted a man, he didn't want me. But a guy I never gave a second thought to—he couldn't get me off his mind. There were eight men in the shop. The younger ones had each given me a quick once-over and instantly dismissed me. The older, broken-down ones were eating me up. I thought one old coot in his barber's smock was going to shave a path right through the middle of his client's natural.

Sim appeared in the doorway then, motioned me back there.

Indeed, Jones did not seem to have much of a sense of humor. But he did laugh at me when I asked if he could direct us out to Waddell's place. He stopped laughing when I dropped my uncle Woody's name on him. He finally agreed to call Waddell and handed the phone over to me. I told the froggy-throated kingpin how grateful I would be for a few minutes of his time.

No, he said. I had it wrong. He'd be grateful for a few minutes of mine.

⑤

THE HOUSE WAS JUST OFF ST. LAWRENCE AT 107TH. A BIG place with two well-groomed, deadly German shepherds in the gated front yard. I left Sim smoking a Newport in the Lincoln.

Waddell took my arm and walked me past a huge front room with clear plastic covering every turquoise sofa, chair, and lamp. It looked frozen in time, and it was appropriately chilly in there. Cold air clawed out at us as we passed it.

"This here is a treat for sure," Waddell said. "I don't get many visits from beautiful young ladies now I'm ah old man."

I laughed girlishly, as if I believed his flattery.

I caught sight of a young man in the kitchen. He had a solitaire game laid out on the table and a black gun a couple of inches to the left of the ace of diamonds. Waddell didn't introduce us.

We took seats in another big room, near the back of the house. This one looked more lived in, and it was heated. I was offered a

drink from a cut-crystal decanter with a little silver tag—
SCOTCH—on a chain around its neck. Identical containers held
bourbon, gin, and so on. I said I'd take whatever Mr. Waddell
was drinking.

Waddell was taken aback to hear that I was one of the hippies
living in that apartment on the North Side where the two kids
were killed.

"What you doing in a place like that? Woody let you stay up in
there?"

"He's never been too happy about where I was living."

"I'm surprised he ain't grabbed you outta there."

"He's about an inch away from doing just that," I said. "I made
a deal with him. I promised him I'd get out as soon as I find—as
soon as the police find whoever did it. But they're looking in all
the wrong directions. They're even trying to blame one of our
roommates for the murder. I'm trying to figure it out some other
way. Just so I know. I have to prove I'm right or prove I'm
wrong."

"Why? Why you doing they work for them?"

"Because the guy who got killed meant something special to
me."

"That was your man?"

"No. But I thought he was great."

I thought he was. Past tense. Suddenly I realized how far away
from Wilton I had traveled in just a few days. Maybe it was just a
matter of knowing, accepting in a way I hadn't before, that he
was dead and forever lost to me. But I don't think that was the
whole answer. Accepting the death meant acknowledging how
far away he had gone from me. What I was remarking on now
was how far away I had gone from him. Curious that of all the
friends and strangers I'd spoken to, it should be Henry Waddell
who triggered this insight.

"Anyway, there's another reason I'm doing their work, as you say. The police are jerking us around. They're playing some kind of game."

"What you mean? They not really trying to find out who killed the boy?"

"I don't know what I mean, exactly. I just know they're doing it. Which brings me around to you."

He popped his eyes. "What the hell I got to do with any of this?"

"Well, as you know, a bunch of us lived together. We had a commune."

"Yeah. Black and white both, ain't it?"

"That's right. One of the guys is the suspect the cops are after—Dan. Another one is an older man. His name is Barry Mayhew. A white guy. I have reason to believe he spends a lot of time on the South Side, back in our old neighborhood. For one thing, he likes the food at Champ's. He's a regular. But I also think he gets the merchandise he sells from somebody in the neighborhood. There's a big market for that kind of merchandise these days. Everybody's doing it."

"Merchandise," he said. "Um-hum." Waddell lit a cigar, and took a much longer time to do it than was necessary.

I didn't wait for him to speak. I went on. "Don't misunderstand, please. I'm not here to pry into your business or involve you in any way. It's just that I'm convinced now that Barry Mayhew's got something to do with those murders. Wait, let me put that another way. In a million years, I couldn't see Barry torturing and killing anybody. Not with his own hands, at least. And he's got an alibi for the time of the murders, anyway. But I think he knows stuff none of the rest of us do—about the killings and about Dan and maybe even about what the police are really up to."

He sat back in his La-Z-Boy, puffed expansively on the cigar.

"Sound like you onto something. Yes sir, I can see Woody didn't raise no dumb children. But what do all this have to do with me?"

"Can you tell me—would you tell me—if you know Barry Mayhew? Was he getting his merchandise from somebody attached to you? And was Wilton Mobley in the business, too? That's all I want to know."

"I'd like to help you out. Out of respect for your aunt and uncle. But all I can do is tell you the way I understand how these things work."

"That's good enough."

"In the business you talking about, there's a big boss and then there's a lot of little men below him. The man at the top got a lot on his mind—deals to make, people in high places to see, wheels to grease all over town. The boss control a lot of money, and everybody want some of it. Man at the top can't be too selfish. He gotta give in order to get.

"But he'll leave the drudgery to the lower men in the company. Kinda like middlemen. They got they own customer bases. White boy doing business up north, he probably selling that mind-changing shit they cook up in labs. But it's entirely possible he's got a source on the South Side for other goods.

"You know what else might happen? A white boy might get to thinking he's a whole lot slicker than he really is. Might get greedy and try to short somebody. Might even try to get himself out of a jam with the law by selling out one of the middlemen. You know, anything's possible."

"So the man at the top wouldn't really know a drone like Barry Mayhew," I said. "Is that what you're telling me?"

"Mighta heard the name somewhere, but he wouldn't know him from Adam. And as for this Wilton cat, your friend who was killed, the boss probably never heard of him until he saw on the news that the boy and some white girl got themselves murdered up on Armitage. So if you think he was doing business with the company, you can forget that."

"I see. All of that makes good sense, Mr. Waddell."

"Um-hum. I figured you'd understand it." He picked up my highball glass, which was still full. "Guess you not that thirsty."

"I'm okay. I'll just nurse this."

He began to chuckle. "Tell me something. I bet Woody got no idea you up here. Am I right?"

"Yes."

"I didn't think so. Way we left it between us, he knew I was entertaining his girl, he probably whip you within ah inch of your life and be talking about trying to kill me."

"He might. But you don't seem too scared."

I watched him roar with laughter, which turned in a minute to thoughtful head-shaking. "Yeah," he said, "old Woody be out-done if he knew I gave you something he couldn't."

"What happened between you and Woody?" I asked then.

"Who you think you kidding, girl? If he wanted you to know, he'd ah told you."

It was time for me to go. I thanked Waddell and rose from the chair. I saw him looking at me, half in the way those old barbers had done.

"You know, you do feature your mama just a little," he said.

"What?"

"I said you kind of look like your mama. I'm telling you, that woman was fine."

The remark staggered me. "You knew my mother?"

"Sure I did. Knew her. Knew your uncle Hero that died. Knew your grandma Rosetta. I know a whole lot about your family."

That expression on his face was meant to intrigue me. And it did. "That puts you ahead of me," I said. "Tell me something else you know about them."

He only laughed, mouth opening like a new wound. "You come around to see me anytime," he said. "I told you, I love to get female company."

WHEN YOU WANT TO PICK UP SIX PAIRS OF CREW SOCKS FOR A buck fifty, or maybe buy a gross of Bic ballpoints for not much more, you go to the open-air market at Maxwell Street. Poor people from every corner of the city flocked there to haggle with street merchants over baby clothes and factory-second brassieres, phony Swiss watches and shower curtains. Black folks used to salivate over the Polish sausages and the foot-long frankfurters the street vendors served up there. Of course, Maxwell Street was the polite term for the hundred-year-old bazaar. But I grew up hearing it referred to as Jewtown. I don't know who coined that nasty bit of anti-Semitism, but the moniker was ancient and ubiquitous.

I fought with myself for only a few seconds before making the call. I was a little confused when Jack Klaus told me to meet him on Maxwell Street. Then he explained that he was going to grab a bite at Harry's, the brightest star in the galaxy of delicatessens in that neighborhood.

I found him wiping mustard from the corner of his mouth. On his plate was a whopping pastrami sandwich and a potato knish big enough to feed the Foreign Legion.

"Have a seat. Hungry?" he asked.

"No. I need to talk to you. Are you eating alone?"

"I usually do. Gets lonely sometimes. I think I remember you turning me down."

"You sound like you're in a good mood, today, Detective Klaus. Very playful."

"Oh, I forgot. Everything's real serious with you. You got an emergency or something?"

"You wanted me to tell you about Barry Mayhew. Well, I have something to say about him now."

"Ah, now you're ready to rat him out. Is that it?"

I was also ready to slap Jack Klaus. But I beat down the impulse and asked if I could have a cream soda.

"Barry hasn't been back at the apartment since yesterday morning. I don't know where he is or what happened to him. But I think he's found Dan Zuni, and I think they both might be in serious danger."

"Oh?"

"Yes. I saw Barry yesterday afternoon, not long after I spoke to you. He was driving Dan's Volvo."

"Very interesting," he said, nodding sagely.

"Did you hear what I said? He was in Dan's Volvo. I thought you were looking everywhere for that car."

"Go on."

"You were right; he does sell grass, and a few other things. He thinks he's the sharp one, likes to treat everybody else like an asshole. But now I think he's in over his head, mixed up with some people who don't play. Barry can be pretty oily sometimes, but I don't want to see him get hurt. Anyway, I'm much more worried about Dan."

"I bet."

"You bet? What the hell is this? You're not really listening to a thing I'm saying, are you?"

"Sure I am. But you can stop worrying about Dan Zuni."

My heart froze. I thought the sadistic bastard was going to tell me I needn't worry about Dan anymore because he was dead.

"Mr. Zuni is safe and sound. We took good care of him."

"You what?"

"He's been in custody since the night of the murders. But he was released a few hours ago."

"You son of a bitch." Tears rose to my eyes. "Where is he?"

"I don't know. But he's a free man now."

I couldn't help letting out a sob.

I guess that touched his so-called heart. "I couldn't tell you, Cass. I couldn't. There's reasons for it, though."

"What reasons? Whose?"

He didn't answer.

"Police bullshit. That's the reason, isn't it? Jesus Christ, I knew something was crazy about the way you guys were acting."

"I have nothing to do with the way this case is being handled. All I could do was try to look out for you a little, to the extent you let me. I'm still not free to tell you why things shook out the way they did."

"Oh, don't worry about it. I'm sure you have a very good reason for throwing a man in prison when you know he didn't do anything wrong."

"Look, I told you. I didn't make that decision."

"Okay, so not you personally. It was that pig Norris who decided. He knew Dan was innocent, though, didn't he?"

"Maybe."

"And now you all are letting him go because you *have* to. Of course. You must have reached some kind of legal limit on how long you can keep a suspect, even a murder suspect, right?"

"Yeah."

"And what about Barry? What's he got to do with this crap?"

"All I know about Mayhew is that he was looking at some serious time on a smuggling charge. Narcotics has been running him for a while now."

"You mean he's a snitch."

"That's right."

"Who's he snitching on? Or for?"

"Not me."

"Yeah, yeah. You don't have a thing to do with it. Your hands are clean. Wow, man, you are something. How the fuck do you live with yourself?"

"Knock it off, Cassandra. I've had enough of you talking to me like that. I do my job and I also try to pay my debts to people. Like Woody. You and your freaky friends hate the police. Well, ain't that too bad. But you know what? You can't make me ashamed of what I do. You get that? I was trying to keep your ass safe, that's all. And this is how you thank me for it."

I hooted at him.

"What's so damn funny?"

"Oh, Klaus. Be sure and let me know the next time you keep me safe, okay? I'll hire a bodyguard. My ass would be dead if I had to depend on you."

"What the hell have you people accomplished that you think so much of yourselves? Oh, yeah. You're gonna stop the war. How's that one coming?"

"Fuck you." I shot out of the chair and nearly knocked it over.

"I should take a belt to you, Cassandra."

"Did you hear what I said, Jack? I said, 'Fuck you.' "

7

"Did you *know*?"

"Woody's not hard of hearing," Ivy said. "I suggest you lower your voice."

I ratcheted it down to a slightly quieter scream. "Just tell me the truth, Woody. Did you know they already had Dan?"

"No, girl. I didn't know they had him. Now, you call me a liar again and see how fast you regret it."

"I didn't call you a liar." Not technically, anyway. I just said I didn't believe him.

My aunt took hold of my elbow. "Cassandra, you are danger-ously worked up. Sit down for a minute and think. You've just been told your friend is not only safe, they just let him go. That's what you want, isn't it?"

I cooled off a little, but still refused to sit. "Of course it's what I want. But it doesn't solve anything, Ivy. It doesn't answer any questions. The police are dragging their feet on this investiga-tion; they're up to some kind of nonsense. It only means we're back where we started."

"No, you're not," Woody said. "You talked to Wilton's people, didn't you? You just flew in here and told us everything his mother said. That's a lot more information than you had this morning."

I had to admit he was right. And I couldn't stand the look of triumph on his face.

"I know how happy it makes you to think Wilt was some kind of bad guy, Woody."

"I'm not happy, child," he said. "I'm a long way from happy. Now, what about the boy Alvin? The Mobleys know who he is?"

"No."

"Then you still got a line to follow. Check him out. You don't know who he is, your roommates don't know who he is, the Mob-leys don't know who he is. What does that tell you?"

"Wilt didn't want us to know him. He had a reason to keep Alvin away from the rest of his friends."

"It seems obvious," Ivy said. "He must be one of the people who were using the Mobleys' property."

"Find him, maybe you'll find out what was happening up there," added Woody. "Or it might work the other way 'round."

"Both those things sound right," I said. "But I have no idea how to do either one of them."

"You'll think of a way," he said. "Just don't go and do anything foolish. Let Jack help you if he can."

"Woody, don't get her started on Jack again," Ivy said. "I just pray the police do their job and do it fast. I want all this to end before Cass gets her neck wrung somewhere."

Yes, that would be nice. Then I could come back home. That's what Ivy meant.

I didn't stay much longer. But before I left I went in and took a fleeting look at my old room, where I'd be living again, soon enough. It meant that living on my own had been a failure. It was going to be like walking backward.

The two of them walked me to the elevator. "Get some rest," Ivy cautioned. "You're all frayed-looking. And have Sim wait until you get inside your apartment."

"I will. But we're pretty protected now. The uniforms are coming and going all the time."

8

I THREW MYSELF ONTO THE SEAT NEXT TO HIM AND SAT THERE brooding.

Sim waited and waited, finally asked, "Where we going now?"

I turned to him. "I'll tell you in a minute. Sim, did I thank you for your help today? I meant to."

"What you doing—you crying?"

"No. Sim, what do you do when you're mad and relieved and sad and . . . and everything you can think of . . . all at the same time? Where do you turn for comfort?"

"I don't know."

I put my hand inside his coat. "Wouldn't you just want to hold on to somebody?"

"Yeah, that's prob'ly what I'd do."

"Don't take this the wrong way, okay? I'm not saying you're simple or anything. But I bet you don't make a practice of complicating things when you don't have to."

"What you talking about?"

"I mean, if a woman let you know she was interested in you, you'd know where to take it from there, wouldn't you?"

"Uh-huh."

"And it wouldn't take you six months to say something if you had a thing for her. Would it?"

"Naw."

"Do you think I'm ugly, Sim?"

"Where you get that? You look okay to me."

"I've got some good-looking grass in my purse. Where is it that you live?"

"West Side."

Gulp. Juvenile gang heaven. "Where on the West Side?"

"Congress Parkway. That where we going?"

"That's where we're going."

9

WE SHARED THE CAN OF MILLER HE HAD IN THE REFRIGERA-tor.

"This is my jam," he said, taking a well-worn record from its sleeve. "You like the Delfonics?"

"I don't know."

"Stylistics? I could play that."

"I don't really know them, either."

"Bet you like Smokey."

"Not really."

"You kidding. How come?"

"Well, they always played the Miracles when the kids were

slow dancing. Nobody ever asked me. I guess it's stupid, but I don't like being reminded. I was alienated."

"You crazy, Cassandra. What you listen to?"

"Hendrix. And I like Beethoven. And Cream."

"Who?"

"Say my name again."

"Cassandra."

Shortly after that, we climbed into his long, plain bed.

Holy Richard Alpert! We were like mating whales.

My aunt Ivy once confessed to being a bit afraid of James Brown. I liked him, but I knew what she meant. However, it wasn't until that evening that I appreciated the profundity of his use of repetition. Namely, *baby, baby, baby*. The same thing with *please, please, please.*

I dozed off with Sim's powerhouse arm across me. Dreamed. Woke. Lay there for a while looking up at the ceiling. I was depleted, but I also had that interval of peace I'd been looking for since the day I heard Clea's terrible wail, when she found Mia's and Wilt's bodies.

I scared the shit out of Sim when I jerked up suddenly and jumped out of bed.

I wrenched my purse from the arm of the chair and turned it out on the plywood table in the middle of the modest room. I pawed madly through all my junk, looking for the silver peace symbol.

Something to remember him by. Hope Mobley's phrase was echoing in my mind. I already had something to remember him by. At least, I thought I did.

I'd been carrying Wilton's keys around with me since the day after the murder. At least, I thought I had.

I had not seen them, as a matter of fact, since that bastard assaulted me in the apartment. I flashed on the sight of my ruined canvas bag slit end to end, contents scattered all over the floor.

Now I knew exactly what the intruder had been searching for, what he stole.

He put me through all that hell for Wilton's keys.

Yes, of course. Keys that fit a door, a strongbox, a safe—or God knew what—but something in or near that house that had passed from one generation to the next of upper-crust Negroes who summered in Kent, Michigan.

10

ONLY A FEW DAYS LEFT BEFORE CHRISTMAS. THE LOOP WAS packed with holiday shoppers.

"You look good, Sandy."

I had to laugh. It was so like Dan Zuni, at a time like this, after what he'd been through, to say something sweet like that.

His eyes were tired, but otherwise he did not look like a guy who'd done three days behind bars. Cliff and I nearly hugged the life out of him.

Dan had called the apartment to tell us he was out of jail— and to say that he was sightseeing with his grandfather, who'd never been to Chicago before.

Sightseeing?

Right, he said. Just released from police custody on a trumped-up charge of double homicide, he was showing his granddad the Wrigley Building and the Magnificent Mile. Wilt was right: Dan Zuni was cooler than any of us.

He asked if we could meet him and the old man downtown; they were going to take the airport shuttle bus outside the Hilton to catch the early-evening flight to Tucson.

"Aren't you coming back to the commune to get any of your stuff?" Cliff had asked.

"No way, man," Dan had said. "The vibes in that place would

bury me now. But you could do me a favor and bring me my tripod."

We didn't just bring the tripod. I packed up his Creedence record, his Polaroid, and the brown T-shirt he loved.

Dan introduced Cliff and me to his grandfather, an ancient-looking version of Dan himself: implacable, with onyx eyes and features carved from granite. It wasn't at all hard to visualize his ancestors picking their way across the mesas, fishing in the streams, worshipping the sun. I didn't know the etiquette; you didn't bow to Indian elders, as you would to the Japanese, but just shaking hands with this living incarnation of history didn't feel like enough of a show of respect. I guess Cliff had managed to overcome his awe of Grandfather Zuni, because after he greeted Dan, he turned to the old man and began to hug him, too.

We must have been about as motley a group as they'd ever seen at the hotel bar.

"I wasn't in the Cook County lockup," Dan explained. "Some guys with heavy shoes had me. I guess they were FBI."

"Feds? They're the ones who grilled you about the murders?" I asked. "Not a homicide cop named Norris?"

"No. Well, maybe him, too. I don't remember all their names."

"But why? What did they want with you?"

"Mostly they were leaning on me about Wilt: What did I know about him, and did he ever talk to me about revolution. Did he have guns in the apartment. Shit like that."

"You're kidding."

"I'm not, man. I swear. A lot of the time they just left me alone. And they kept giving me steak and french fries for dinner. I don't even like steak. I mean, once in a while it's okay, but I'd rather have spaghetti—or that eggplant that Mia used to make. That was my favorite."

Planet Zuni. Taylor's description of Dan's world.

"It sounds like the federal clowns just wanted to stick you somewhere, take you out of commission for a few days. And when they were good and ready, they let you go."

"That was the trip," he said. "They gave me back my Leica, but they kept the film."

Grandfather Zuni was knocking back a second Jack Daniel's, telling a rapt Cliff about his early life on the reservation. I slid off the bar stool and took Dan by the arm, led him back to the gents' bathroom.

I locked the door behind us, handed him the joint I knew he was hankering for, passed the book of matches to him. "Okay, Dan. Talk quickly, before somebody comes in. You and Mia."

He looked down briefly, then back up at me. "There was a baby. It was sad."

"I can imagine. But I don't mean that. I mean before. You and Mia were together before she knew Wilton?"

"Yes. We lived in the building across the street."

"Not Crash and Bev's building?"

"Yes. For almost two years."

"And Wilt knew?"

"Sure. He was okay with it. Besides, he had a right to know."

"And were you okay with it?"

He smiled. "I loved Mia. And I loved Wilt. And together they were—" His voice gave out there.

That was an awful moment. All this time, I'd felt sorry for Dan because of what the cops had put him through. Now I realized that because of that ordeal, he'd had no time to feel the weight of the loss of his friends. He had been given no time to grieve.

He cleared his throat. "So you found them, right? You saw them—dead."

I nodded, heard the choking noise he made. "Go ahead," I told him. "It's okay to cry."

"No," he said. "Not now."

I waited a long time for him to speak again.

"I should go now, Sandy," he said finally. Then he stubbed the joint out on the bottom of his shoe.

"All right. Just one more thing. How come Barry's got the Volvo?"

"He asked to borrow it for a couple of days. To do some business, he said. He laid some mescaline on me for it. I said sure, just gas it up when you're done."

"Oh. That's not such a big mystery at all, is it?"

He kissed me on the forehead. "Tell him it's his now."

"If I get the chance."

"If what?"

"We haven't seen him for a couple of days. I'm thinking . . . well, what difference does it make now? I'll tell him."

Cliff and I, both teary-eyed, watched as Dan and his grandfather found seats on the bus.

"Don't forget us, man," Cliff called.

Dan gave him the peace sign. And then he lifted his Polaroid and aimed it. He took our picture.

CHAPTER SIX
SATURDAY

①

I DID MISS HYDE PARK, IN A WAY. IT HAD AN AUSTERE BEAUTY in the cold. The streets on the North Side were so much noisier, and no whispering trees towered protectively over the houses.

I passed Toad Hall, the electronics store where I'd bought a radio with my birthday money the year I turned fifteen; Jimmy's Bar, the old beatnik hangout where the poetry readings with bongos took place at night; the used-book store, where as a twelve-year-old I regularly made a pest of myself with the owner, Mr. O'Gara.

Woody and Ivy always had lunch out on Saturday afternoon, after they took their walk. They either went to Valois on 53rd Street, a cafeteria with a long steam table, or to the Medici, a little café where UC students sat reading for hours, and where they served the "espresso scrambled eggs" and warm Italian bread that Ivy and I loved.

I caught up with them at Valois. As popular with cabbies as it was with coeds and librarians and retirees, the place was busy and loud. I pushed my way past the crowd at the door and joined my aunt and uncle at their table.

No, no, no, I didn't want anything to eat, I told them. I wanted their help. Obviously Jack and his cop friends don't give a damn about who killed Wilt, I said. Now that I had put together the meaning of Wilton's keys, I knew they had something to do with the murders.

"Cass, you can't just invade those people's property," Ivy said sternly.

"I know that. But I've got to figure a way to get a look around up there in Kent."

"It's damn sure Oscar Mobley's not going to let you do that," Woody said. "You said he wouldn't even tell his own wife what he found. What are you planning to do? Just go up there and boldly let yourself into that man's house with his dead boy's keys?"

"I don't know. I might've tried that. But I don't have them anymore."

"What happened to them?"

I was going to pick the moment to tell them about the break-in. But it looked as though the moment had picked me. "Listen. I may as well tell you. There was a little trouble—a little more trouble—at the apartment."

Ivy dropped her soup spoon into the bowl.

"Calm down," I said. "It's all over now."

"What trouble?" Woody demanded.

"Somebody was waiting for me when I got home a couple of nights ago. He roughed me up, took off with those keys. I didn't want to tell you because I knew how you'd react. Exactly like you're reacting now. But he didn't hurt me. He got what he came for. The keys. Don't you see? That's why he left the minute he found them in my bag. That's why nothing else has happened."

Ivy pushed her soup away. "Oh, Lord. Don't you care anything about your safety, child?"

"Yes, I do, Ivy. You're not the only one who doesn't want me to get my neck wrung."

I dared to look over at Woody then, dreading his gaze. "I have one thing to say," he pronounced. "And I'll only say it once. Sim will be going with you when you go back home. And he will stay in that apartment until you move out. I don't expect to hear any argument, understand? Because if you say one word, let alone try to refuse . . . I'm through. Through with it all. No more help. No more information from Jack. No more money. No more tuition. Nothing. You understand?"

"Yes."

What else was I supposed to say? God had spoken.

I looked away from him and over at the trio of cops on the food line. They eyed our table as they ordered great tongue sandwiches, soup, and cream-lathered desserts. I knew it must be snowing again. Their shiny blue jackets were wet, the imitation beaver collars slick and ratty-looking. But the hungry cops would have to wait for an empty table. Uncle Woody was nowhere near finished talking.

"I don't understand you, Cass," he said. "You must get some kind of satisfaction from living this kind of life. But I'm damned if I know what it is. Who are these people to you? Why do you stay up there with them after all this mess has happened? What'd they ever give you?"

"They liked me, Woody."

"That is the stupidest thing I've ever heard," Ivy said acridly. "Why don't you tell the truth? You just want to be cut free to misbehave, without us watching you. You'd rather smoke that stuff and roll around with men than tend to the business of getting an education and taking your place in the world. Don't you understand, Cass—you are needed. Young people like you are the only hope we have as a people."

I couldn't speak for a moment. Wilton had related the gist of numberless such lectures he'd received from Oscar Mobley. The difference was, I was too gutless to make some smart-ass reply.

So I was supposed to restore hope among my people. That was a tall motherfucking order, and I wasn't even remotely up to it. Goofy, neurotic me, leading the race on to glory. No problem. I'm right up there with Sojourner and Malcolm and Booker T. They used to throw temper tantrums and hide whole German chocolate cakes under their beds, too, didn't they? And eat LSD like it was salted peanuts?

I finally said, "When this is over, I'll try to do better. I'll apply myself better. Is that okay?"

They both had locked jaws and teeth.

"Like I said, I've a favor to ask. Another one. Will you do it, Ivy?"

"Me?"

"You. Help me this one last time. And then I'll try to be more like you want me to be."

"Oh, the hell you will, Cassandra."

"Will you?"

"Yes, girl. What is it? Just tell me. And then go on out of here before I lose my mind."

②

SIM WAS ONE OF THE LAST PEOPLE I IMAGINED FITTING INTO the mix at the commune. And where was he going to sleep? I had an image of his huge feet hanging over the edge of the sofa. But then I realized there was no shortage of beds now. He could bunk in Annabeth's abandoned room, or in Dan's, anywhere but Wilton and Mia's bed. That would be ghoulish.

He dropped me at the apartment and then went home to pack a few clothes, and maybe a couple of his LPs.

Before I left Valois, the venerable Woody had dispensed some more sage words. "Look through the boy's belongings," he said. "You may notice something nobody else would pay any mind to. Maybe you'll be the only one it means something to."

Good thinking. The problem was, I'd already done that. Most of the knickknacks in Wilt and Mia's room had belonged to her— Hopi Indian dolls, yoga mat, jewelry, sewing baskets, that kind of thing. Wilt had little besides his clothing and the secondhand bicycle his boss at the shop had given him.

He didn't have any other belongings except his books.

Then look at those, Woody instructed.

That idea didn't sound so wise to me. In fact, it sounded dumb. I did it anyway. Nothing to lose.

"But they're mixed up with everybody else's," Cliff pointed out when I enlisted his help.

"Yeah, you're right," I said. "But it's not going to be as hard as it sounds. Barry doesn't have any books. Annabeth wasn't much of a reader, either. Dan doesn't have anything but art books. And all Taylor's books are out on the sunporch. So that leaves Wilt and Mia, me and you. You know what's yours, I know which ones are mine. That whittles it down a lot, right?"

He shrugged and started thumbing through the ones on the top shelf. We encountered *Alice's Adventures in Wonderland,* I. F. Stone, *The Doors of Perception,* Richard Brautigan, *Nine Stories,* Eldridge Cleaver, Tolkien, Ken Kesey and *Dune,* Adelle Davis, *Goodbye, Columbus,* James Baldwin, Ross McDonald, *On the Road,* and Lao-Tse. Dog-eared volumes we'd passed back and forth, special editions from our childhoods. But no cryptic messages in any margins, nothing more interesting than a grocery list or movie showtimes jotted down inside a cover.

Some 250 books later, we gave up. I turned on the TV set, expecting to see Cronkite, or as Taylor called him, Uncle Walt. We had to settle for whoever it was anchoring the Saturday news. The reports from 'Nam were as scarifying as usual.

At the commercial break, something on the TV stand caught my attention. A burst of bright yellow on a dark background. It was the illustration on *The Wretched of the Earth*. I blew the dust off the cover and opened the book. In the middle was a folded sheet of ordinary white paper. I opened it out and saw it had a kind of letterhead: two hammy black fists, a grenade in one, an ugly-looking bowie-type knife in the other, and underneath them, the word TURNABOUT in thick black letters.

I held it out to Cliff. "What's that?" he said.

"I have no idea. Doesn't exactly look like an invitation to a garden party, though."

I refolded the paper and replaced it in the book, then took them both to my room.

"I think I found something," Cliff called to me a few seconds later.

He was in Annabeth's old room, picking through the few odds and ends she had left behind. He was holding a couple of sheets of typed text. The pages were messy, sentences had been partially erased, corrected, scratched out. The words didn't make much sense at first. But then I spotted my own name. And Cliff's name. And Annabeth's. And the word *murders*.

I had to read it over again before the pieces fell into place. "Oh, Christ," I said. "It's a story. About us."

"Who's writing a story about us?"

"I don't mean a short story. It's some kind of report—about the killings and everything else about all of us. We have our own little Hunter Thompson in residence, remember."

"Taylor," he said.

"Yeah. Taylor. He's writing about us for *Rising Tide*. Do you love it?"

3

TAYLOR WAS WEARING A SHIRT AND TIE WHEN HE CAME home, a marked change from his usual Army-Navy store duds. Ordinarily we might have needled him a little about the job interview threads. Not today. We pounced on him.

"You're being a little melodramatic, Sandy. I'm writing about the commune and the murders. I'm not 'betraying' you guys."

"Then how come you never told us what you were doing?" Cliff asked.

"I was going to."

"Yeah, right," I said.

"I was, man. I'm at the point now where I'd like to interview everybody. Before we all—you know. Lucky I got Annabeth to talk before she split."

"Let's see the rest of it," I said.

"What?"

"Let us read what you're saying about us."

"Well, no."

"Why not?"

"Look, Sandy, I'm a journalist. I'm entitled to write about what happened. Don't get so uptight. I'm not saying anything bad about you. In fact, you're one of the stars of the piece. Your background makes you really interesting. That, and the way you're obsessing about Wilt."

"Is that so? I'm glad you think I'm so fucking interesting, Taylor. Do you think Wilt's death is interesting, too? Jesus Christ, man, he was supposed to be your friend, not your big break."

"Do me a favor, okay?" he said. "Just wait till you read it. Maybe you won't be so judgmental then. Hey, look—Cliff, you're not mad, are you?"

He wouldn't answer. He just stood there with the typewritten sheets pointing at Taylor like an accusing finger.

Taylor looked relieved when he heard the knock on the front door.

Oh, right. It was time for them to meet Sim.

DINNER WAS "INTERESTING," TOO, IN A KIND OF ABSURD WAY. I cooked, so the food was pretty awful. Cliff ate nothing, but must have downed a six-pack of Heineken. Taylor kept asking if it was all right to interview Sim, whom he kept referring to as my bodyguard, which annoyed the hell out of me.

After supper, Uncle Woody phoned and asked pointedly to speak to Sim, not to me. Guess he was still pissed off. I talked briefly to Ivy, though, who had already started delivering on the help she had promised to provide.

Before I went to bed, it occurred to me that Taylor's expertise in the current political scene might come in useful. I got the piece of stationery with the two black fists and showed it to him.

He shook his head. "I'm not sure, but I think I might have seen this logo somewhere," he said. "It means something. I just don't know what." I was about to leave when he added, "But you know who might?"

"Who?"

"Your friend Nat. Either him or that guy who's always with him at the Wobbly hall. Torvald."

I imagined De Lawd would not be happy to have me contact him about something other than us—our relationship, that trite, overused word. My apology to him would have to be abject. If he wanted me to fall on my knees before him, I knew I'd have to do just that.

I had a hot bath, smoking and soaking in the tub for almost ninety minutes. By the time I dried off and changed into my night things, the house was quiet and dark. I got into bed, rolled another skinny joint, tried to unclog my mind. Nat was part of the logjam. I kept going back to the time line of the murders, thinking how Cliff and Mia were probably getting slaughtered while I was at Nat's place. Thinking, too, about my shame at suspecting even for a moment that Nat could have been my attacker.

All kinds of images floated in and out of my head as I was drifting off to sleep: the table radio back in my room at Woody and Ivy's; the beautifully browned cornbread Nat had made for me; the brass ashtray on Jack Klaus's desk; three Chicago PD officers in dark blue jackets, looking like fat birds on a telephone wire; Annabeth's lovely hands sorting Indian cotton blouses; the comfy leather chair in the Mobleys' drawing room; the peace sign on Wilton's key ring; the buttery yellow of Sim's shirt collar peeking out of his jacket; Henry Waddell's obscenely wet lips.

But just before I fell off, I heard a muffled commotion in the hall. When I snatched the door open, I saw Sim, in pajama bottoms, and Cliff, in long johns, both reaching for the knob to my door.

The three of us stood frozen for a minute, nobody saying a thing. I merely closed the door quietly, and turned the lock. Then I pulled the covers way up over my head.

CHAPTER SEVEN

SUNDAY

THE LAST ONE TO GET UP, SIM STILL LOOKED SLEEPY. HE found us in the kitchen, all dressed and in our coats. "Y'all going to church?" he asked, rubbing at his eyes.

"We're going out for breakfast," I said. "And then I've got to go see somebody. Although church doesn't seem like such a bad idea at this point."

It took Sim a few minutes to notice Jordan, who was staring up at him in wonderment, as though he were looking at a brown bear in a bathrobe. "This is a little friend of ours from the neighborhood," I explained. "We're going to get him some pancakes. Jordan, say hello to Sim."

The boy wouldn't speak, though. He just looked down shyly at his galoshes and moved closer to Cliff.

"There's nothing to eat here," Taylor said to Sim. "If you want, we can bring something back."

"Naw, I gotta go with y'all. Mr. Woody said I should stay close."

We waited downstairs while he dressed. The street had that enchanted feel to it, soft, heaven-sent snow beginning to blanket everything. But that's the kind of weather that's dangerous in Chicago. While you're distracted, thinking how lovely it is, the whole city shuts down, traffic paralyzed, kids lost in snowdrifts, old people dying in their lonely rooms, riots over the last quart of milk at the corner store. We'd had a blizzard last year that blew every other one off the books.

Taylor and I watched as Cliff and the child made snowballs and frolicked in that Norman Rockwell kind of way.

"Go long!" Cliff shouted to Jordan as he backed away, lengthening the distance between them.

Taylor gave me a cigarette. "So we're okay again? Friends?" he asked. "Or do you still think I'm ripping you off?"

"I guess we're okay," I said. "Anyway, what difference does it make what you write about us?"

"Far out. Do you think your grandparents would talk to me, too? You know, background stuff."

"Jesus. How long is this article going to be?"

Before he could answer, I heard Cliff's insistent cry. We looked up the block to see him signaling madly. Taylor took off, with me not far behind.

Cliff was scratching and pawing at a parked car, wiping at the coat of snow on the windshield.

"Goddamn," Taylor said. "It's Dan's car."

The driver door wasn't locked. Some loose coins and an empty cigarette pack were on the floor in front; a few old newspapers, candy wrappers, a tire iron, and a dented thermos on the backseat.

"Try the trunk," I said.

Taylor worked at the lock with one of my bobby pins, but he couldn't manage to spring it. We searched for a sharp instrument to try jimmying the lid, but the snow hid all the usual street detritus. Finally Cliff took the tire iron and hacked at the trunk until the lock popped.

Taylor's voice was agonized: "Jesus! No!" he cried, and let the tire iron fall at his feet.

Rank air shot out at us like a hand from the grave. Jordan tried to step closer, but Cliff prevented him. I saw him scoop the boy up roughly and send him running.

Inside the trunk, Barry was folded into himself like one of those trick collapsible cups. He was blue-gray with death. His lips were horror-show black, and so was the hole under his ear. I fell away from the sight of him, screaming. Cliff held me fast in his arms. The tighter the better, I thought, because otherwise I just might break apart.

Sim was rushing toward us by then.

"Never mind!" I shouted at him. "Get Woody! Just go!"

②

"NICE OF YOU TO BRING US IN ON THIS ONE," DETECTIVE NORris said. "I hear you think you know more about police work than we do."

I offered no lip. In fact, I was prepared to be downright contrite, until he snarled at me, "What you ought to be thinking about is getting yourself a lawyer."

"Why? I didn't kill Barry. And I'm not the narc who let my snitch get killed, either."

"Keep it up. Bury yourself some more."

"Why not just frame Dan Zuni for it? It worked the last time."

"You meddling little snot. You've interfered with this investigation from the word go. I'm coming after you. I don't care how connected your nigger granddaddy is."

There. It was said. I grinned at him, picturing him with his eyes gouged out.

Taylor was staring at Norris with loathing. "I heard what you said. I'm a witness, man."

"You better shut up, sonny, if you don't want to find yourself in lockup for the night," Norris answered.

"Intimidation, too. Just you wait," Taylor said. But Norris never heard him. He had turned and walked back to the Volvo.

Jack Klaus was on the scene as well. He was keeping his distance from me. I saw him exchange a few words with one of the men from the medical examiner's office as he and another guy lifted Barry's body into their van.

"I guess we're the main attraction at the carnival again," I said to Taylor. "But what do you care? You're probably thinking about that Pulitzer you're going to win."

"Why don't you cut it out, Sandy? How'd you like me to write about your asshole behavior? And how totally wrong you were about shit."

"What shit?"

"You keep saying that nobody is out to get the rest of us. Even after you got jacked in the apartment, you refused to believe we're all at risk. You said the murders were all about Wilt. Everything that's happened was just about him. Well, what is this? A coincidence? Your little theory is shit, isn't it? There *is* some crazy out there who wants to kill everybody who lived in that apartment."

"No, Taylor, there isn't."

Klaus walked up then. No greeting. All business. "They need your statements. They're going to take everybody in."

"Fine," I said. "Who gives a fuck? I've got a statement you all can take right here." My voice was loud and belligerent, like a thousand fed-up women I'd seen drunkenly telling off some man. Norris snapped to attention.

Cliff stepped up close to me, tried to take my hand. "You'd better be cool, Sandy. Don't make it any worse. Please."

I shook him off. "It's okay," I said. "First of all I've got a question for Massa Norris."

"You speak when you're spoken to," he said, fuming. "You don't have a question for nobody."

"Yeah, I do. How's Annabeth Riegel doing? She tell you everything you need to know?"

Klaus and Norris exchanged looks, but neither said anything.

"What kind of trip are you on, Sandy?" Taylor asked. "What does Beth have to do with anything?"

"Beth gave you a nice interview, huh, Taylor?" I said. "I can imagine. And then she got out before you tried to contact anybody from her family. She split in a real hurry. But not because of that fight we had. And not because she was so terrified of getting got by the big bad serial killer. She had to get out before you realized she was phony."

"Phony?"

"You heard right. Annabeth was some kind of plant, Taylor. She's a police informant. The Riegels who have all the money, the ones who live in Kenilworth—they don't know Beth from Janis Joplin. My aunt Ivy made a couple of phone calls to some of her lady friends. One of them is on some committee with Mrs. Riegel, and she has no daughter. Beth is not the heiress to a meat-packer's fortune. If she's not a cop herself, then she's a police spy, and a damn good one.

"Not only was she tracking every one of us, her job had her dealing with freaks day and night. She might overhear just about anything. I bet she was real curious about the haps at *Rising Tide*. You guys are always doing exclusive interviews with fugitives the FBI is looking for, people going underground, or their comrades or their families. You write about people who cook acid and speed. You've got sources inside the police department telling you about the bad shit the cops pull on us. You must have been a gold mine of information."

I gave Norris another million-dollar smile. "You're not writing anything down," I said. "Don't you want to get my statement right?"

Jack Klaus would not meet my eyes.

I looked at Norris again, using my words as if they were spitballs. "You'll correct me if I get anything wrong, won't you, Norris?"

No answer.

So I kept going. "Who owns that farmhouse that was supposed to belong to Annabeth's father? Is that a property the bank took away from some poor dairyman? Or maybe the FBI uses it for interrogations. Do they take people up there to sweat them? Come on, Norris, you can tell me. Am I being too fanciful here? Maybe it just belongs to your old aunt Ethel, huh?"

I turned to Taylor then. "You know what my aunt would say if she could see you now, Taylor? 'Close your mouth, dear, before you start catching flies.' "

He began to sputter. "You're telling me that Beth—I mean, all that time—everything she said—"

"Yeah. All lies. The only thing she didn't lie about was being an actress. Pretty brilliant acting, the way she was all worried about where Dan was, when she knew all along the police had him. Dan was just a pawn in some big game. The real target of whatever the game was, was Wilton. That's who Beth was really watching. Except I don't know why."

"That's right," Norris said. "You don't. You don't have the answer—for a change."

"Maybe not. Not yet. But let's hear your answer to this, you bastard. You know very well who killed Wilton and Mia. And if you say you don't, you're a damn liar. Go ahead, deny it."

Jack looked genuinely shocked at that last bit. He waited for Norris to speak, incomprehension in his eyes.

"I don't have to tell you shit," Norris crowed. "It's time for you to shut your fat mouth." He beckoned to a couple of uniforms. "Put her in that unit over there," he said, "before I knock her down. Take them all in."

Jack Klaus was white with tension, and feeling very caught, I imagined. He didn't dare take my side against Norris. But on the other hand he must have known I'd tell Woody how he let Norris treat me.

Following the boss's lead, the cop in the blue zippered jacket handled me as roughly as he could. He didn't really hurt me, but when he shoved me into the cramped backseat of the squad car, the snow that had collected on his fake fur collar splashed me and I let out a cry.

Not a cry of pain, though. Like I said, I wasn't hurt. I had just realized something that made too much sense not to be right. I knew then that the man who had tied me up in the apartment had been wearing a Chicago PD uniform.

③

I WAS ALL SWOLLEN, MY THROAT SORE, EYES BURNING. I SAT in the back of the Lincoln, between Taylor and Cliff. Uncle Woody rode up front, next to Sim.

I guess it was kind of funny. Cliff, Taylor, and I had done nothing wrong. We merely reported finding a dead body. But Dan Zuni, supposedly a murder suspect, had probably been much better treated than we were. Hour upon hour at the station house, we were given no food, nothing to drink, no air, no breaks, and made to stand for long periods or sit on back-killing hard benches. I bet they'd have kept us all night—hell, if Norris had his way, they'd have just taken us out and shot us—if Woody and his attorney hadn't shown up.

Woody took us to the all-night diner on Belden. There was a trippy symmetry in that. The Belden Deli was exactly where we were headed that morning, before Cliff spotted the Volvo.

We ate like wolves. I polished off three waffles and enough sausages to fill a sidecar. Taylor finished an enormous hot roast beef platter and then, while he waited for a second one, tried to interview Woody. I thought at first that Cliff was too shell-shocked to eat, but when his bacon cheeseburger was set in front of him, he devoured it just as greedily as the rest of us were eating, and followed it with two helpings of cherry pie.

Over coffee, I put the picture together for Woody and the others. The cops, ably assisted by Annabeth Riegel, were running some kind of surveillance operation on us, with special focus on Wilton. I remembered that Jack Klaus, that first day I'd gone to see him, had called Annabeth just "Beth." He'd shortened her name in the same overly familiar way he always called me Cass, like my family did, like he knew me. That had stayed with me ever since, way at the back of my mind.

The night of Wilton's and Mia's murders, the cops pulled Dan Zuni in for questioning; they knew he was innocent, but for some diversionary reason, they decided to keep him under wraps, pretend they were still hunting for him over the next three days. That same night, they picked up Barry Mayhew, only they let him go. Because he was a known informant and they had other plans for him.

"And how did he get hold of Dan's car?" Taylor asked.

"That's no longer a mystery. The explanation's pretty simple. Dan just lent it to him that morning, and none of us knew about it.

"At any rate, a couple of days later Barry was bopping around the South Side. I spot him and think he's hiding Dan. But that isn't it. He's probably doing drug business. He's in hot water with the police. They're using him to gather evidence against some bigger fish. Could be he was wearing a wire or setting them up in some other way. But his South Side drug connections were onto him, and they killed him."

Woody was watching me, his eyes narrowed. Trying to prevent him from asking me about drugs and the South Side, I started talking faster. "I'm speculating here," I said. "But it does add up, right?"

"Yeah," Taylor said, "it does. But it doesn't seem like Barry's got much to do with the Wilton thing. So go back to him and Mia."

"Right, Wilt and Mia. A nice white girl from a good family and the son of a prominent black attorney—true, they're not Mayor Daley's kids, but there's got to be some pressure on the cops to solve the case. Why haven't they made any progress? Because they already know who killed them. They're just waiting to make an arrest, stalling."

"Stalling for what?" Cliff said.

"I don't know that yet. I only know it's tied in with the reason they were spying on Wilton. They're about to drop a big bomb. And they must be close, damn close to doing it. That's why Norris is so furious at me for getting in their way."

"You say the police must know Wilton was carrying on some kind of monkeyshines up in Michigan," Woody said. "How do you figure that?"

"Because of the keys. Some key on Wilton's key ring opens something up in Kent."

"Lot of trouble to go to for house keys," he said. "Why not just break down the door or go in through a window?"

"I don't know. Maybe the key isn't for the house. Maybe it's a safe-deposit box at the local bank. Who knows? I just know the man who assaulted me and took those keys was a cop."

"You'll never be able to prove that, Cass. You didn't see him. Besides, anybody could've been wearing a jacket like you talked about."

"I know. But I'll bet anything I'm right. Who else could have had such an easy time of it? Just slip into the building and wait for one of us to show. For days after the killings, there were uniformed officers all over the neighborhood. One of them was told to get those keys, but not to hurt anybody in the process."

I don't know if Woody was buying everything in my version of events, but at least he was firmly back on my side. And he was in a cold rage about Norris being so filthy to me. I knew he would figure a way to get even with him, which made me really happy.

"WHAT IS THIS PLACE?" SIM ASKED.

"The Wobbly hall," I said.

"Wobbly?"

"Industrial Workers of the World. They're anarchists. You know—Joe Hill and all that."

He still had no idea what I was talking about.

"Like a labor union, but more than that. It's complicated. Just wait down here. I won't be long."

On the way up the stairs, I thought about the Halloween party Nat had taken me to at the hall. I went as Emma Goldman. We drank jug wine, listened to Paul Robeson 78s, and sang "Solidarity Forever" about a hundred times.

The place was as ghostly as ever. Glorious old bowed windows, greasy with dirt, looking onto Lincoln Avenue. Rickety wooden chairs thick with dust in neat rows facing a makeshift stage. Except, few of the meetings or events at the hall drew enough people to fill even a quarter of those seats.

Nat was standing across from his friend Torvald at one of the long tables. They were collating mimeographed pages. Tor saw me before Nat did, and raised a welcoming hand.

Nat stared at me for a long moment. There didn't seem to be much anger in his eyes anymore. What was I seeing there instead? Perhaps just indifference.

I kept a few feet of space between us. "Hi."

He didn't respond right away. But then he said, "Tor, can you excuse us for a minute?"

"No, don't," I said. "I was hoping to talk to both of you."

That made Nat a little suspicious. "What about?"

I handed over the single sheet of stationery I'd found in Wilton's copy of the Fanon book. "Any idea what this is?"

He looked for a minute at the two black fists in the logo, then up at me. Then he passed the paper to Tor.

"August 4," Torvald said.

"What?"

"The August 4 Committee." I guess he thought that was an explanation.

"They're Vietnam vets. They're a service organization for guys who come home from 'Nam."

"Is that all?" I said.

Tor cast a quick look over at Nat before speaking again. "Not exactly."

Nat spoke up finally. "They're a covert group, Cassandra. They organize to get black soldiers to desert or defect to the Cong."

"I see. So what does that word under the drawing mean—*Turnabout*?"

"I don't know. What are you doing with that flyer anyway? You about to take up arms now?"

"No. I—I found it."

"And that's all you came here for? Satisfy your curiosity?"

"No. Not really. I have more than that to say to you."

He waited. But I didn't speak up. "Guess you don't have more to say, after all."

I looked at Tor then. "Maybe you could give us a minute alone."

He backed away.

"You're making this hard, Nat. Which I understand. I do, really. But I'm trying to do something here that's pretty important."

"Trying to find out who did Wilton in."

"Yes."

He shook his head in disgust. And for a second there, my fondest wish was to be a Bengal tiger, because I'd have leapt on him and clawed him to death. But I managed to push that impulse down. My God, I thought I had stopped resenting poor Nat for being alive. I guess I hadn't yet.

"Look, Nat. I actually just want to ask you to forgive me."

"That was nasty, the way you acted, Cassandra."

"I know it. Inexcusable."

"I thought me and you were—"

"We weren't, Nat. That's what you wanted, but we weren't."

"Sure, you're right. We couldn't have much of anything together as long as Wilton was alive. Now he'd dead, you're more in love with him than ever."

I knew for a fact now that wasn't true. But I let it stand.

"And the useless cops still haven't found who did it?"

"Oh, yeah," I said. "They know."

"So how come you're still asking questions?"

"It's too hard to talk about now. I have to go soon," I said. "Maybe we'll get together sometime. As friends, I mean."

"Maybe."

"How are things going with the free school?"

"Okay. Still got that picture of you one of the girls drew. It's up in the coatroom."

I had helped Nat when he first organized the free school/preschool. Most of the children were needy and sweet, and some of them had already been plowed under at age four or five.

"Thanks for the info," I told him as I left.

"Watch yourself, Cassandra."

"What are you talking about?"

"Just watch it. You messing with something you have no business doing. Think I don't know you at all?"

On the way out, I called my thanks to Torvald, who told me to wait just a minute. He brought me a thin sheaf of papers wrapped in tissue. "Little present for you," he said.

I removed the wrapper, saw what he had given me: the new anarchist calendar for the year ahead. It was a little beauty featuring an exquisite line drawing for each month and noting the milestones in leftist history for every day of the year. Tor had been hand-lettering and reproducing calendars for years. Nat's collection of them dated back to 1951. I thanked him for the gift as I flipped through it quickly. March 7, 1942—Lucy Parsons dies. April 6, 1931—the trial of the Scottsboro Boys begins.

2

I MADE OUT A LITTLE IN THE FRONT SEAT WITH MY CHAUF-feur, then he drove me over to the *Rising Tide* office, where I figured one of Taylor's co-workers could help me with some research on the August 4 Committee.

The office was a mile-high mess of manuscripts, empty soda bottles, denim jackets, LPs, manila folders, ashtrays, books. I could smell traces of tacos and grass as I walked past the empty receptionist's desk.

Actually, just about all the cubicles were empty. On the one other occasion I'd visited Taylor on the job, the place was wild with activity. Where was everybody? I made my way back to the big space the staff used for meetings. I found them all watching television in a kind of group trance.

An assassination. *Another* one. These days, that was the first thing you thought when you saw a crowd of people staring intently at a TV.

But that wasn't the explanation.

A daytime TV series about vampires, called *Dark Shadows,* was hugely popular with heads. In fact, a lot of Debs College students who were hooked on it would flock to the Sears Roebuck just across Wabash Avenue to catch it every afternoon. Sometimes the electronics department in the store was so jammed with freaks, the straight people couldn't even move.

But no. The *Rising Tide* people weren't grooving on that vampire soap opera, either. They were looking at the local news, and a few people were booing the face in close-up. Taylor grabbed me by the arm and pointed me toward the screen. The star of the show was our own vampire-torturer, Detective Jim Norris.

He was announcing proudly the breakup by authorities of a dangerous cadre of radicals. The black man found shot to death several days ago, who had rented a transient apartment under the fictitious name of Larry Dean, had now been identified as one Alvin Flowers.

Flowers, the ring leader of a group that aimed to foment revolution among black servicemen, had apparently been killed by another member of the group.

"Bullshit," Taylor said. "I bet the cops killed this Flowers guy in cold blood."

There was a chorus of right on's from the staff.

Two core members of this group, calling itself the August 4 Committee, had been apprehended as they attempted to leave town by bus, Norris said. The group was wanted by the feds on sedition charges. Moreover, they were responsible for a string of murders from Maine to Louisiana.

Murder. The blade or the grenade, I thought. Whatever will kill. Turnabout. So this Alvin Flowers was Wilton's hero, the authentic black man who was so outtasight.

But Norris wasn't finished.

He took my breath away with the next part: This same Alvin Flowers, he said, was behind last week's shocking hippie murders in a North Side apartment. Authorities had determined that Wilton Mobley, a member of the August 4 Committee, had defected from its ranks, so his colleagues had assassinated him to keep him from informing on them. Mobley's female companion, Mia Boone, had been an innocent bystander.

"That's ridiculous. Wilt was in some outfit that was fucking killing people?" Taylor said. "What a load of crap."

He was vibrating with righteous indignation. I wasn't. I was hollow, speechless.

"I underestimated you, Sandy. You're good."

I looked back at the television, saw a preening Norris. "So are they," I said.

"Who? The cops?"

"Yeah. I wonder if they murdered Wilt, too."

3

THE NEWSPAPERS HAD THE STORY BY NOW. ALL THE DETAILS.

No justice. No beauty. No truth.

In my dirty room, I was affirming those words, droning them

like a mantra. I was also trying to obliterate the reality of them with marijuana and music turned up so loud the jars on my bureau were dancing with the vibrations. But it wasn't working.

I was still fully aware that the police were pulling off an outrageous cover-up, and they were probably going to get away with it. They had tied things up so nice and neat: Wilton was part of August 4 and he wanted to pull out. So Alvin Flowers killed him . . . but oops . . . an innocent white girl got in the way, so she had to die, too.

And who killed Alvin? One of his comrades. Why? They'd argued over money, that's why. The white comrade, Paul Yancy, had over $100,000 in his duffel when he was apprehended at the Greyhound bus terminal.

Yes, all of that would hold together when they railroaded this fall guy Yancy.

Cliff had been knocking at the door to my room every five minutes for the last half hour, but I refused to answer. Finally he barged in and snatched the plug to my radio out of the wall.

"Get your ass off the floor," he screamed at me. And when I didn't move, he took me by the shoulders and shook me.

I had provoked another mild-mannered guy to near violence. Great. I might not be slinky, but I did have a certain power over men.

"I'm getting out of here, Sandy. I've had it. I'm withdrawing from school and I'm splitting."

"So go."

"I want you to go with me."

"The only place I'm going is Hyde Park."

"You don't have to, and you know it. Are you coming with or not?"

"Fuck off."

His face crumpled.

"I'm sorry, Cliff. But just leave me alone."

"I can't."

"Why not?"

"Because I love you. Why do you think?"

Tears welled up inside me.

He nearly crushed me. "Let go, Sandy. You have to let go. They're gonna beat you if you try to take them on. You already proved how tough you are. Let Wilt's people fight them."

"They're not going to fight for him. They believe the cops. So do Woody and Ivy. 'Cass, you're being ridiculous. We haven't come to the point where police come into our homes to murder us.' That's what my aunt said. I didn't know whether to laugh or cry. Everybody believes the fucking cops. You probably believe them, too."

"No. But what are we going to do about it?"

I hung on to him. "I don't know," I said, and let the tears come.

I didn't know whether I loved Cliff, either. But when I had dried my eyes, I said, "You want me to go home with you? What's your mother going to say?"

"What do you mean, because you're black?"

"Well, yeah."

"She's not like that. We're not like that."

Nobody—not even Nat—had ever held me that way and told me they loved me. What did you do when that happened? You said yes to them, didn't you? Even if you weren't sure you loved them back.

"But why do we have to go to Connecticut?" I said. "Why can't we get a place here?"

He searched my face. "Is that what you want? You mean you'd live with me if I stayed in Chicago?"

"I'd think about it. Yeah, I'd think about it seriously. And you wouldn't have to leave Jordan, right?"

He smiled then. "No, I wouldn't have to leave Jordan."

"At least nobody's got to be afraid anymore," I said. "You know what I mean?"

"Yes. Nothing else can happen now. Everything's already happened."

We sat in the dark for a long time. "Cliff?" I said. "Put the radio back on. Low."

"Okay. But I want to know something first."

"What?"

"That guy Sim is gone. And Taylor's working all night."

"Yeah?"

"Will you sleep with me tonight? I mean the whole night."

"Yes."

"Good, that's what I want," he said. "And call your aunt Ivy."

"What?"

"She called you before. But you wouldn't open up."

I shook my head. "That can wait. I know what she wants: When will I be coming home?"

CLIFF WAS SO SWEET, AND APPARENTLY KNEW EXACTLY WHAT he was doing. We made love all night. He didn't rock me to my foundation the way Sim had, but we made a good fit. Instead of hollering and sexy talk, we soothed each other.

While we rested in each other's arms, he made a lot of promises and asked a lot of questions. I felt like there was almost nothing I couldn't tell him. He got the Book of Cassandra in installments; I'd talk, we'd make love again; talk, do it again.

"I used to be so jealous of you and Wilt," he confessed.

"Really?"

"Yes. I know it went against everything we were all supposed to be like. But I couldn't help it."

"But Wilton was never in love with me. You knew that."

"Yeah. Maybe. But you had something with each other that you didn't have with anybody else in the commune."

"Because we're both—were both—black, Cliff. That's not hard to understand, is it?"

"I guess not. But I still hated it. I hate everything about being black or white that keeps us in these boxes, separate and ignorant. It's poison, the race thing. If we don't find a way to get over it, it's gonna kill everybody."

"Amen to that," I said.

"We're going to take one step toward solving the whole thing," he said.

"What step?"

"Kids. You know. Children. Medium brown."

"Cliff," I said in wonderment, "it takes you a while to make a move, but when you do, you don't play."

"Who was the Bible guy you and Wilt used to talk about?"

"Bible guy?"

"Yeah. All you had to do was mention it, and the two of you would go apeshit laughing."

"Oh, him. The Read Your Bible guy. He was a nut who used to preach at the el stop at 63rd and South Park. 'Read your Bible. Ask the Lord for the understanding. And he will give it to you.' It was all he ever said. He was around when I was ten, and he's there to this day. Wilt used to see him, too. The guy must be a hundred years old by now, and the last time I got off the el at that stop, he was still there."

"I want some secrets with you, too," he said. "I want to have some things we can laugh about someday."

"Maybe we will, someday. We sure have enough to cry about, don't we?"

WHEN I AWOKE AT FIVE IN THE MORNING, I WAS SO FOGGY I could barely find the floor with my feet. I had smoked an awful lot of grass. And now I was ravenous.

The linoleum floor icy cold under my bare feet, I dug around in the fridge until I found a yogurt, carried it into the front room. Sunrise. I remembered the morning I'd watched the sun come up at the Wisconsin farmhouse. We were having such a great weekend. Why had I felt so funny as I stood alone in the attic? Then I remembered. It had something to do with Wilton. But then, everything did. Let go, Cliff had said. Jesus God, when would I be ready to let go of Wilt?

That weekend, he had been morose one minute and then hyper the next; angry, then calm, then jubilant. Somehow, I didn't think it was the drugs.

I'd never seen him dance so much. He and Clea were putting on a real show, teaching the others how to do the old dance step called the roach.

"What's got into you?" I said. "I thought you said all you wanted to do up here was sleep and eat gingerbread."

He was grinning from ear to ear. "I just worked out my Oedipal thing," he said. "I figured out a way to castrate my pop. I'm going to slaughter that pompous prick. Squish . . . Squash . . . yeah, baby. Kill that roach!"

The others screamed with laughter. In their cases, it definitely was the drugs.

"What the hell are you talking about, Wretched?"

"Oh, don't worry, don't worry, sweetheart. I just mean metaphorically. You know what brother Oscar say: Each man kill de thang he love."

I did have to chuckle at that line. "Brother Oscar" was Oscar Wilde. But Wilton's dad was named Oscar, too. When I tried to question him again, he wouldn't let me talk. "Get your ass in gear and dance, girl."

"Yeah, that's right," Clea said, pressing herself against Wilt. "Get those big titties out here and show us what you got."

An hour or so later, I caught a glimpse of him in the bedroom he was sharing with Mia. They were on some old cushions on the floor, his head in her lap. She looked up at me and smiled, then pressed a finger to her lips. Shhhh. He was sleeping.

Now, how do you castrate, kill a man like Oscar Mobley . . . metaphorically? He was rather small in stature, nothing to look at, but proud of his accomplishments and his place in the community. If you wanted to ruin him, what did you rob him of? His reputation, his dignity, his money? All of which he had in abundance.

I was yearning for a cup of coffee, but I didn't make any. I thought the aroma might wake Cliff, and I needed more time alone to think. Also, I knew how unhappy he'd be to find me still trying to unknot the facts surrounding Wilton's death.

Hope Mobley had told me that Wilt and his father were arguing bitterly the last few weeks. She'd hear snatches of the fights they were having behind closed doors. Wilton was doing something that threatened Mobley's law practice. Isn't that what she thought she heard?

Position. Dignity. Money. Most things came down to money, didn't they? That was what we abhorred as a generation. We hated living in a world where money came before human life, before principles, before loyalty, honor, law. Some people say the civil rights movement is being bought out with money. Some were saying—notably a Chicago PD detective named Norris— that money was at the root of the murder of Alvin Flowers, head of the rogue organization called the August 4 Committee.

Money. Was it really that crude, that simple?

I found that piece of cheap paper with the August 4 logo. I turned it over and began to sketch something from memory, a dim memory to be sure, almost like automatic writing: the shape of a thick, oddly shaped key.

I DRESSED WHILE I DIALED THE NUMBER AT WOODY AND IVY'S.

"Cass, why are you calling so early? It's barely six o'clock."

"I'm sorry to wake you. You know when I asked you to do something for me a few days ago? You found out about the Riegels for me."

"Yes."

"I need you to follow through on the second part of that favor. Now."

I heard a sigh of exasperation. "Jesus Lord, Cassandra. You're not still harping on that house in Kent, are you? And the stolen keys? I did everything you asked me to do, child. I went to the funeral and spoke to Hope Mobley. Now the truth has come out about her son. If she can accept it, why can't you?"

"I'm not going to bug her, Ivy. I just want to give her something."

"What?"

"Something that belonged to Wilt. I'm sure she'd want to have it. I just need you to call and ask if she could see me for a second—without her husband knowing about it."

"Her husband?"

"Yes. He wouldn't appreciate me dropping in there again."

"Goddammit, Cassandra, why can't you leave the poor woman alone?"

"Will you do it? Please. I won't ask for anything else."

"At six in the morning, girl?"

"All right. Wait until seven."

"Cass, have you packed up—"

"Thanks, Ivy. See you later."

I'm a terrible girl. Lie. Lie. Lie.

CHAPTER NINE

TUESDAY

I WOKE SIM UP, TOO. I HADN'T FIGURED ON SEEING HIM AGAIN this soon. But I needed him.

He didn't pick me up in the Lincoln this time. He was driving borrowed wheels. We stuffed our faces with sweet rolls and store-bought coffee while he drove south.

Maybe it was the maid's day off. Hope Mobley opened the door herself this time. And this time I could see Wilton in her more clearly. She had his eyes and forehead and his tawny coloring.

"Cassandra," she said. "You have a pretty name. I thought if I ever had a girl, I might name her that."

"I'm intruding again," I said. "But I wouldn't do it if this wasn't important."

"I'm sure you think so. Your aunt told me how much you take things to heart. I like her."

She caught me peeping around the big entrance hall. "I understand you're worried about seeing Oscar. Don't be. He isn't here."

"Oh?"

"No. He's at the Drake. Until we can decide what our future will be. Whether we have different futures, I should say. You don't have to stand in the doorway, either. Come in. You have something for me, I believe."

With no further explanation, I took out my mammy-made sketch, handed it over. "Is that something you recognize?"

It took her a minute. "I believe so. But what on earth is the meaning of this?"

"What does it open, Mrs. Mobley?"

"This is too much."

"Please tell me."

"A kind of safe house. A bomb shelter my father insisted we install up at the house in Kent. My God, that was years ago. But how do you know about this key?"

"Wilton had it."

"Wilton had it? But why? I mean, he couldn't have. There are only two copies of this key. Mine is in a bureau drawer somewhere and Oscar's is in his desk."

"I bet one of them is missing."

She took a step away from me then, suspicious. "Whose secrets are you trying to get at, young woman—Wilton's or Oscar's?"

"I don't know. Maybe both. I'm not out to trash anybody's memory. But I'm not going to stop until I know what went down."

"No, I guess you won't. But isn't it time you let them rest—my son and the girl?"

"You think they're resting? They're not."

I couldn't stand the look on her face, and hated myself for putting it there.

"Go and look for the keys," I said. "Please."

②

SIM DROVE STEADILY AND FAST, AT LEAST FIFTEEN MILES over the limit. Hunched over the wheel, he was an odd mix of relaxation and attentiveness. More like a fighter pilot than a guy ferrying a lady to the country.

For a few minutes I let myself pretend I was Hope Mobley in better days, when her prosperous, lucky family was young and together. A lovely young wife on a leisurely car ride to her country place.

It was one in the afternoon when we left the highway and pulled onto the road heading north. We stayed on that until we reached the rough, rock-strewn one that led to the house.

The Mobley place stood at the end of the path; it was big and lonely looking. The wood on the upper story was splintering from wind damage, and the place needed a paint job.

"She said it's past the house," I told Sim. "About a half mile west of here. This way."

He followed in my footsteps. "Why is it so far away from the house?"

"They told Oscar Mobley it should be built near some natural shelter, so he had it installed close to the dunes. To dilute the shock waves from the nuclear blast—would you believe? I guess that's how people were thinking then. They expected Russia to try to wipe out the state of Illinois. Hope said she told her father it was preposterous, but he wouldn't listen."

The terrain became hilly, and soon we had entered what looked like an old creek bed. "There," I said. "It should be about a hundred yards from here."

I started to walk fast, and within five minutes we were staring at two moldy steel doors lying flat to the ground.

Oscar's key. Hope's key. The issue was moot now. We didn't need one. The doors were flung open. We looked at the gaping blackness they bracketed.

"What you think is down there?" he said. Neither of us wanted to be the first to descend into the unknown.

Finally Sim made a move. He took the first step down the wet stone staircase. Once we were at the bottom of it, we could see nothing.

"There's gotta be a light," I said. "Feel around for it."

All at once, a string of lights popped on. He'd found the switchplate.

The inside of the chamber was like an oversize sardine can. The space was rectangular. Two doors at the far end—toilets, maybe. Cabinets on the wall. A camp stove. Bottled water in one corner. Propane canisters. Fire extinguisher.

And on the ground, close to the stairs, was an upended Mosler safe. The door to that was open, too, and the safe was on its side.

"That belong to the husband?" Sim asked.

"Good bet."

Sim bent to inspect it. "Yeah, look," he said, pointing to three small holes near the tumbler. "This sucker been drilled open. Wonder how much green was in this mother."

Only then did I begin to notice the trash on the floor. Beer and soda cans and balled-up waxed paper, a dozen cigarette butts. There was also a folding table and a few wooden milk crates that had obviously been used for seating.

Sim was motioning to me. I joined him at the far corner of the chamber, where he was using the toe of his boot to poke at the three duffel bags lined up next to one another like mushrooms at the base of a rotted tree.

"Army issue," he said.

I tipped one over, undid the elaborate rope knot that fastened the duffel and began to shake out the contents. The clatter was so loud I jumped away in alarm. But then I could see they were just rods of metal and wood. "What is this junk?" I said.

Sim seemed to be intrigued with the stuff. I went about opening another duffel while he got down on his haunches. When I looked up a minute later, Sim was no longer squatting. He was on his feet, and he was raising the business end of a semiautomatic.

I fell away from him, shrieking. "What the fuck are you doing? Where did that come from?"

"What you called the junk in this bag. I just put it together. Nothing to it."

"How do you know how to do that? You were in the army?"

"My brother was. Korea." He spread the bag open for me to look inside then. "There's five disassembled carbines in there. Plenty of ammo, too. Even a few smoke grenades. Somebody was expecting company down here."

There weren't any guns in the second bag. What we saw when we emptied it were telephone books for a variety of American cities, road maps, manila folders with densely scribbled notes inside them.

I opened one of them, spread the pages out. I saw the word COPY stamped across most of the sheets. Sim was reading over my shoulder. "This doesn't make any sense," I said.

"Yeah, it does. It's a DD-214."

"A what?"

"A soldier gets one when they discharge him. That's your service record. You need it to get a job after you get out of the army."

"Like I said, this makes no sense."

One of the maps was for Lincoln, Nebraska. There was another for Shreveport, Louisiana. But not all the maps were for your typical American town. I was holding a hand-drawn one, done in colored pencil, almost childlike. It was shaped like a giant fantail shrimp. Here and there on the map were crosses and notations.

"You know what that is?" Sim asked.

I nodded. "Yeah, I do. It's Vietnam."

That third bag was the kicker. The end. When Sim turned it over and shook it, nothing came out at first. So I reached in. I felt the slick surface of the material, pulled at it. A dark blue jacket with a heavy zipper and a fake fur collar plopped out of the duffel. The collar wasn't the only fake thing about the garment. A badge was on the front of the coat. I wasn't an expert on police gear, but the metal seemed too lightweight to be real. A fake Chicago PD shield.

I was holding it in my hands, but I could feel the slick, wet surface of that jacket on my neck and face, scent the breath of the big man who'd mauled me in the apartment that night. And I felt the powerful hand in the small of my back as I was shoved into the closet.

I flung the coat onto the ground. Sim was now shaking other items out of the duffel. A couple of dozen pamphlets featuring the August 4 logo flopped out. And there were several photos of white men, some young, others older, some in uniform, some in civvies. But the notes written on the back of each shot told me all the men had been U.S. Army officers: name, rank, length of service, company, unit, date of discharge, where in 'Nam each had seen action, last known address in the States.

I had them all spread out, looking in vain at each face for a clue as to why they were in that bag. One of them began to speak to me a little. I flipped his photo over and looked at the data on him. And yes, there was a DD doohickey for him, too.

A sourness shot up from my stomach then. I could feel the poison in my throat. I leaned forward, sick and rattling like a teacup on its saucer.

"**Drive faster**," I said.

"No, I'm not gonna drive no faster. You better get a grip on yourself."

"I'm in a goddamn grip," I said. "I'm just about being stran-gled."

"Dig, Cassandra. The guns, that writing and stuff—looks to me like you found proof everything the police say is the gospel truth. Your boy Wilton was in with those people. They had ah arsenal in there. Of course they the ones who took all the money his daddy had in that safe. Of course they woulda offed him if he was gonna inform on them. Just like the cops announced."

"Yep, so it seems." I was not going to argue with him. "As a matter of fact, I was wrong to blame the department for a lot of the stuff that's happened. They're just a bunch of choirboys really, trying to keep the city safe."

"What you looking like that for? You sad 'cause it turns out your boy was a bad motherfucker?"

"Yes," I said. "And no."

4

Sim parked in front of our building.

"You'd better not come upstairs with me," I said.

"Why? I thought—"

I saw the disappointment on his face. He had been expecting another afternoon of dynamite sex, dynamite reefer, and Mo-town sounds.

"I know. You thought you'd be grooving with me. Not this time."

"Oh. Okay. But why you was in such a hurry to get back?"

"A funeral," I answered. "I didn't get to go to Wilt's. Wouldn't want to miss this one."

"Say what?"

"Nothing, Sim. I better go." I kissed him then. "Thanks for all your help."

"Cassandra, you are one crazy broad."

"Bye, Sim."

"Look here. Where can I get some smokes around here?"

"Turn left at the corner. There's a store next to the Cuban restaurant."

After he was gone, I stood in the street, looking up at the apartment window above the commune. The room where Wilt and Mia died. It was just as Cliff had said: Soon we'd all be leaving the big noisy apartment on Armitage. No matter what was waiting for me down the line, I knew that the six months in the Armitage Avenue apartment would loom large, stay with me for all my life. I ached and sorrowed for my friends Wilton and Mia, and even for Barry.

The apartment was warm and friendly-feeling when I finally went inside. Cliff and Jordan were drinking cocoa and playing dominoes at the kitchen table.

Cliff rose to give me a kiss, proprietary hand running down my arm. He even unbuttoned my coat for me. "I missed you. Why'd you take off like that, before I got up?"

"I was shopping for your Christmas present," I told him. "It's a surprise."

"You're kidding."

I shook my head. "No," I said, and placed the glossy photograph of Lieutenant Cary Tobin, Cliff's older brother, on top of the domino game.

I watched the smile on his lips fade to nothing. "Where'd you get that?"

"What happened, Cliff? Why did you do it?"

"Jordan," he said woodenly. "Go back with your dad now, okay? I'll come get you in a while, buddy."

I watched in silence as he argued and cajoled and finally barked at the kid to make him go. Jordan was blubbering, but finally he did leave, the front door slamming shut behind him.

He wasn't the only one crying. Cliff was leaking tears as well.

I walked over to him and slapped him with all my strength. "You killed them, didn't you? You slit their throats. And somehow it's all tied up with your brother. Isn't it?"

When he didn't answer, I walloped him again. "You *fucked* me, Cliff. You killed my best friend and then you fucked me."

"I love you." Voice atremble.

"You say that again and I'll kill *you*. Tell me what this is all about. Now."

"They murdered Cary," he said.

"August 4, you mean. They killed your brother."

"Yes. He didn't die in 'Nam. They killed him at home, in Bristol, four weeks after he got out of the army."

"Why?"

"There was a racist group among the officers in 'Nam. Some of them were in the Klan. They had this conspiracy to get black GIs. These officers would send them on suicide missions. Some of the black troops were out-and-out murdered, but the white guys made it look like they were killed in action. All kinds of horrible things were done to those soldiers. Out of hate. Resentment and hate.

"Alvin Flowers was over there. He knew what these white officers were doing. When he got out of the army and came home, he started this movement, August 4. They were trying to get black servicemen to desert, refuse to fight for America. That's what they said they were about. But they were also tracking down the racists—and paying them back."

"Jesus. And your brother was one of the racists?"

"No."

"What do you mean, no? If he didn't do anything, why should the August 4 people kill him?"

Cliff began to laugh then, hopelessly. "They made a mistake. Alvin Flowers and his people had to have inside help. Somebody who could send them army records, keep them up-to-date with who was getting sent home, where people lived, and all. There must have been a mix-up somewhere, though. Cary got marked as one of the racists, and the August 4 people killed him. They killed him for nothing, Sandy. For nothing. My mom didn't raise us to hate anybody."

It was an ugly story. I figured any explanation was going to be ugly. But this was the worst.

"How did you find out about August 4? And where does Wilt come in?" I said. "How'd you know he was a member of August 4?"

"He wasn't."

"What?"

"Not a real member, I mean. I came home one day, before you moved in. Wilt had a black guy up here. They were talking in his room. I didn't know who he was, but I heard Wilt call him Alvin. After the guy left I saw some papers and a pamphlet that told about the so-called mission August 4 was on. I tried to get Wilton to talk about it, but he wouldn't. And I never saw the guy again.

"I followed Wilton all over the city sometimes. But I could never catch him with Flowers. I guess Flowers had gone underground. You were living here by then.

"That weekend we went up to the farm, when Mia was doing all her cooking, she and Wilt thought they were alone in the house one afternoon. But I heard them talking. He told her everything. He said he wanted to join Alvin in the radical work he was doing, but he didn't feel like he was enough of a man to kill anybody, even a racist bastard. So he was helping August 4 in the only way he could. He was letting them use his parents' property and he was giving them money."

"Money he took from his father."

"Yes. Wilton said he'd found out his father had money hidden all over the property, a fortune. And he'd learned the money was dirty."

"Dirty how?"

"I don't know. But he said he was going to take it away from his old man and use it for something the old man would hate. He was going to make a fool of him. It would be poetic justice. He laughed about it."

Yeah, he did laugh.

"What else did you hear, Cliff?"

"That Alvin Flowers knew how hot he was. The feds were looking for him, the Chicago pigs, too. He was holed up in an apartment somewhere, and he and his men were going to be splitting soon. That's when I knew; if I was going to catch him, kill him, I didn't have long to do it."

"So. That day," I said. "The day you murdered them."

"I didn't exactly have it planned. But the time just seemed right. We all ate lunch together. Dan was out. Barry came and went real fast. You split to go see Nat. I told Wilt and Mia I was taking Jordan out sledding.

"Mia had a class. That herbalist course that she went to. I knew it lasted two hours. I sat in the window at Jordan's place, watched Mia leave the building. I knew Wilton was alone. I went back to the building and up to the vacant apartment. Then I called him up there. Just to look at the space, I said."

"He was kind of surprised when you tied him up and started slashing his throat, I imagine."

He looked away from me.

"Didn't he fight you at first? What? Did you have a gun?"

He nodded. "It was the one he got for protection. But he promised Mia he'd get rid of it. He never did, though. He gave it to me to hide for him."

So Wilt also had a little taste of poetic justice before he died.

"How could you do it, Cliff? How'd you get yourself to kill him? He was our friend."

He began to weep again. "I know that. I know that. I just wanted him to tell me where Alvin Flowers was. I had to make him tell me."

"He wouldn't, though."

"No."

"And then it fell apart even more, right? When Mia came back unexpectedly."

"Yes. I don't know what happened. Maybe she forgot something. Maybe the class was canceled. But she walked in on it, started screaming. I had to shut her up. Before I knew what was happening, she was dead."

"So then you had no choice. You had to go through with it and kill Wilton."

"That's right. I had to."

I heard the insistent rapping at the front door then.

"Beat it, Jordan!" Cliff screamed. "Go home like I told you."

"Cassandra? You okay in there?"

It was Sim.

Cliff was faster than I. He snatched a chef's knife from the drainboard and then grabbed me up. "Don't touch that door, Sandy."

"Why? You afraid of what he'll do to you?"

"I don't give a shit about that. I hope he kills me."

"I hope he does too," I said. It just came out of my mouth automatically. A second later, I knew I didn't mean it. "Let's end this now, Cliff," I said. "I'm letting Sim in here. And you're not going to do anything to stop me. Or are you? Are you going to hurt me, Cliff? Cut me up like you did them? What was all that shit about loving me and taking care of me and brown babies? All bullshit, right?"

"It wasn't, it wasn't. I never bullshitted with you. Don't you think I realized we didn't have long? I just wanted to be with you for a while. I wanted to show you, even if Wilt didn't see you for who you are, I did. Even if he didn't love you . . . I did."

Sim was pummeling the door now, kicking at it, grunting. Cliff made a crazed rush forward and threw it open.

But Sim was no longer there. Uncle Woody was. His camel hair coat parted like a theater curtain on the black heft of a sawed-off shotgun, which was leveled at Cliff's heart.

Cliff gave me one last backward glance, and then raised the knife and stepped toward Woody, delivering himself.

The blast took Cliff's arm off at the shoulder.

I dropped right where I was. Just fell on my ass, screaming out his name.

Once again, I had a friend's blood on my shoes. Only this time I could take no refuge in memories from happier times in the past. Nothing existed now but the present moment.

CHAPTER TEN
VALENTINE'S DAY, 1969

SPIRIT-KILLING COLD IN CHICAGO. BUT I WAS WARM ENOUGH. Ivy had given me a sheepskin coat for Christmas. Some Christmas it had been: Ivy, Woody, and me around that underdecorated tree, a tar baby angel watching o'er us as we opened presents in our bathrobes. I'd never been happier to see the holidays come and go.

I held on to Owen's arm as we made our way along Clark Street. We were still friends, thank God. Maybe even closer than we used to be. But somehow we didn't feel the need to talk as much as we used to when we were together.

Owen's coat, I kept telling him, really wasn't warm enough for Chicago winter. He didn't seem to care that much. He wasn't even wearing a hat. I guess the whiskey kept him warm, and besides that, he was always happy when he saw old Mae West movies. That's how we'd spent Valentine's Day, seeing the double feature at the Clark. I had no sweetheart and neither did he, so why not?

The commune murders and the August 4 debacle were still very much with me. A couple of pieces of the puzzle were still missing, and might remain that way forever.

I knew, for example, that the man who'd tied me up in the apartment had been Paul Yancy, the white member of August 4. He'd posed as a cop, taken the bomb shelter key. More than likely he was the one who drilled into Oscar Mobley's safe and took all that money. But had Wilt promised that fortune to August 4, or had he had other plans for it? And was Yancy planning to turn it over to the remaining members of August 4? Or did he get greedy and decide to keep it for himself?

I spent a lot of time thinking about that money. Dirty money, Cliff said. How did it get so dirty? What was the prestigious Oscar Mobley doing that nobody but Wilton knew about? I couldn't cast him in the role of a Mafia hit man or a sleazy black-mailer. But as one of the high-placed citizens above reproach who took bucks from a man like Henry Waddell? As Waddell himself had told me, anything was possible.

Last, Cliff died before I got to ask him something: If Wilton never cracked under torture, never told him where Alvin Flowers's apartment was, how did Cliff track Alvin down and kill him? My best guess is that he didn't.

I think the murder of Alvin Flowers was the one killing the cops really did commit. Just as Taylor had said. Maybe his article would be published and blow the lid off the whole filthy cover-up. Maybe. More likely, though, it would be seen as more left-wing conspiracy paranoia.

One thing involved no guesswork at all. I knew it for a fact and I had never wavered from it: Wilton wasn't killed because he sold out Alvin Flowers. I now realized he was killed because he re-fused to sell him out.

Turnabouts. There was no end to them.

I live alone now and that's kind of okay. I don't mean literally alone. I'm back at Woody and Ivy's place. But I have my own little universe there. My room, my radio, my books. I miss hearing laughter down the hall, passing a J back and forth, sitting down to meals with a crowd of pretty young people, striding on the street in formation with them, the mean north wind whipping hair into our eyes.

"Did you hear me, Cassandra?" Owen asked.

"No, sorry. I was somewhere else for a minute there."

"I said, What are you smiling about?"

"Something that happened once. A bunch of us from the commune were on the street one day. This stoned-out young girl comes running up to us. She's smiling like the Maharishi and her eyeballs are these whirling little pinballs. Anyway, she looks at us and says, 'Oh, wow, man! You guys! You guys are *beautiful,* you know? You look like the Mod Squad.' "

"The what?"

"Oh, for God's sake, Owen. The TV series."

"Ah."

"Anyway, we start cracking up, right?"

"Why?"

"Because the kids in the Mod Squad are undercover cops. This spaced-out little hippie chick thinks we're beautiful 'cause we look like the pigs."

He tried gamely to share in the joke, but clearly it meant nothing to him.

In another minute, he asked, "Should we go right up here to Wells Street for a drink? Or should we walk back to my quarter and go to Otto's, where the stout is better? Don't you think?"

I took his raw, reddened hand and shoved it in his coat pocket. "Owen," I said, "you're the teacher."

AUTHOR'S NOTE

I have exercised the author's privilege of intermixing fact and fiction. Some locales in Chicago—head shops, restaurants, bookstores, and so on—have been given slightly different names. Occasionally I have fudged the geography of some South Side and North Side locations. And Forest Street, where Cassandra lived as a child, is wholly imaginary.

ABOUT THE AUTHOR

CHARLOTTE CARTER has worked as an editor and as a teacher. She is the author of the Nanette Hayes mystery series (Warner/Mysterious Press) and the novel *Walking Bones* (Serpent's Tail). She is a longtime fan of mystery fiction and film noir. She lives in New York City.

ABOUT THE TYPE

Caledonia was designed by William A. Dwiggins in 1939 and originally appeared under the name Cornelia with the Mergenthaler typesetting machine factory in Berlin. Conceived as a reworking of the Scotch Roman which was designed for Mergenthaler Linotype in New York, the neotransitional Caledonia has serene, vertical forms, unflexed serifs, and a transitional style italic. Linotype reworked the typeface in 1982 and released it as New Caledonia. This large typeface family is perfect for large amounts of text due to the fine weight differences it allows. Caledonia's cool, classic look can be used for almost any application.